Dear Santa,
    For Christmas I want
to be a family again.

            Your friend,
            Chisty

DAD→ ☺☺ ←MOM
      ☺
      ↑
      Me

Dear Reader,

Little Christy Holt is the wiliest seven-year-old ever to hit Mistletoe Mountain! Last month she brought together a most unlikely couple, and this month the mischievous miss turns her twinkling eyes on her estranged mother and father. We're delighted you could join Christy for the second book in THE LITTLE MATCHMAKER duet.

Author Jule McBride lives in Pennsylvania, where she is a full-time writer. She burst on the romance scene in 1993 when her first book, *Wild Card Wedding*, won the Best First Book award from *Romantic Times*. She's been a reader favorite ever since.

From Christy, Jule and all of us at Harlequin, we wish you a New Year filled with happiness!

Sincerely,

Debra Matteucci
Senior Editor & Editorial Coordinator
Harlequin Books
300 East 42nd Street
New York, NY 10017

Santa Slept Over

JULE McBRIDE

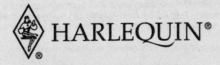

HARLEQUIN®

TORONTO • NEW YORK • LONDON
AMSTERDAM • PARIS • SYDNEY • HAMBURG
STOCKHOLM • ATHENS • TOKYO • MILAN • MADRID
PRAGUE • WARSAW • BUDAPEST • AUCKLAND

ISBN 0-373-16757-1

SANTA SLEPT OVER

Copyright © 1999 by Julianne Randolph Moore.

Prologue

Christmas Eve, 7:00 p.m.
Holiday Hamlet, N.C.

What if Santa won't help me? Christy Holt thought. "Oh, quit projecting," she whispered aloud and then added, "Deep breath." Dutifully drawing in a deep, fortifying breath, the seven-year-old slowly exhaled. There. She felt better. "*Mucho* better," she added, now practicing her Spanish.

But what could be holding up Santa? All evening, Christy and the other kids had been waiting. And waiting. But now her time was running out, since a uniformed deputy—probably one who was trying to help find her parents since she was a runaway—was making his way across the ballroom of the charming old inn.

Christy's eyes darted past him, settling on the costumed party-goers mingling near Santa's empty throne. Christy sure wished he'd hurry.

What if her parents were found before she could talk to him? As it was, her mom thought Christy was spending Christmas in Los Angeles with her dad, while her dad thought she was in New York with her mom…and boy, Christy sure didn't want to be there when they found out she was really in Holiday Hamlet, North Carolina. If the deputy found them or figured out Christy had been giving the sheriff false leads before she got to talk to Santa, there'd be you-know-what to pay.

The well-being of her whole family was as stake.

"Deep sigh," she whispered, reminding herself not to dwell on the negative. She should be concentrating on only one thing—meeting Santa Claus. Of course, he might refuse to help her since she'd had doubts about believing in him, or because she'd been such a bad girl this year. She was always getting grounded and having her phone privileges revoked, and last week, her pet snake had caused a ruckus, nearly getting Christy's mom fired from her job…

"Here he comes!" someone shouted.

Finally. Whirling around, Christy ran with the other kids to the windows. Blowing out another frustrated sigh, she tugged anxiously at the green tights to her elf costume and peered into the white-yellow halos that ringed the old-fashioned iron lamps along the inn's stone walkway. Stars were scattered above the dark, snow-blanketed mountains, and the man in the moon smiled down while white flurries danced in the liquid night sky.

Christy moaned. "Where's Santa? I don't see him."

''There, hon.'' Adult hands settled on her shoulders, gently turning her and redirecting her attention. She gasped. An ornate golden sleigh was skimming over the snowy hillside. Was it the real Santa, or one of those fakers, like the one she'd seen at Bloomingdale's in New York before she'd run away?

''Real reindeers,'' she whispered approvingly when the sleigh drew closer. Squinting harder, she scrutinized the snowy white beard and how fat he looked under the velvet, fur-trimmed robe he wore with his suit. He definitely *looked* authentic.

''Ho, ho, ho!'' he boomed, waving as the sleigh circled past the windows. ''*Meeeee-rrry* Christmas!'' Reining in the animals, he brought them to a halt. As he stepped from the sleigh, snow swallowed his shiny black boots, and a second later, he swept inside the inn.

Hanging back, Christy watched as grown-ups began marshaling the kids into a line. What if Santa wasn't merciful? What if he said she'd been bad, which was true, and denied her only request? Still, rumor had it that when Santa came to Holiday Hamlet, every child was granted his or her wish— no exceptions. Which was one of the reasons Christy had run away and come here. Sure, she might have been bad. She might have stolen some lollipops, or sneaked down the fire escape so she could play in the park, but from here on out, she'd be a model child if Santa granted her wish.

"Whoops!" she suddenly whispered, seeing the deputy come toward her again.

"Relieved sigh," she added when he stopped to chat at the drink table. "That's good." But now Christy wished she'd gone first. Santa was taking his time, and the line of kids was moving so slow. Inching forward, she told herself once more that she didn't *look* naughty. She'd given herself a fresh manicure, with blue sparkle nail polish, and she was wearing a cute elf outfit and her best black patent leather shoes. Santa was no dummy. One look— and he'd realize Christy had reformed.

Santa winked and crooked his finger.

Gulping, Christy glanced around. She was still the last kid in line.

"C'mon, Christy," Santa called out. "As much as I'd like to wait, I've got a long night ahead of me, as you can imagine, what with flying all around the world, to France and Spain and—"

Christy didn't hear another word. Her lips parted in amazement. It had to be the real Santa; he knew her name! And he was right. Here she was, thinking only of herself again, and forgetting that Santa had lots of other kids to see. How could she be so selfish? What must Santa think of her?

"*Mama mia,*" she whispered in Italian. And then she swiftly ran up the stairs and across the stage to the throne, emitting a gasp as Santa scooped her onto his lap. "So, you're the real Santa, right?" she managed to say, after dispensing with a few preliminaries. Only the real Santa could grant her wish, since it was such a doozy.

Santa squinted. "The *real* Santa?"

"Not like the ones at the shopping malls and Bloomingdale's?" she clarified.

Santa scratched his beard, then finally settled on saying, "Well, Christy, I figure I'm as real as it gets."

It wasn't as much assurance as Christy had hoped for, but it would do. Shimmying up, she cupped a hand around her mouth and whispered, "Good. 'Cause, see, I don't want any toys. I just want my mom and dad to get married again. They're divorced right now, and it's not working out so good. Mom cries sometimes when she doesn't think I see. And Dad's... Well, anyway, can you do it, Santa? Can you get them married again?"

Behind his round wire-rim glasses, Santa's eyes widened, making Christy feel pretty sure he was wishing she'd asked for something easier, like cheerleading pom-poms or a Giga pet. As he scratched his beard in contemplation, the moment stretched into the longest of Christy's life. The pressure became so excruciating that she couldn't stand it anymore and slid off his lap.

"Whoa there, Christy—" Santa ineffectually snatched at the back of her elf costume as she ran for the edge of the stage.

Knowing she had to try one last time, she whirled toward Santa. "Is it 'cause I've been so bad this year?"

"No, of course not, but—"

"Then it's 'cause you plain don't like me?"

"No, Christy, but—"

"Is it 'cause you're just mean then?" she probed, feeling tears sting her eyes. When he didn't answer, she raised her voice, no longer even caring that all the other kids were listening. "If you're the real Santa Claus, it should be easy. All I want's for my parents to get married like everybody else's!"

For such a big man, Santa looked strangely helpless. Then he said, "Uh...don't worry, kiddo."

"Does that mean yes?"

Something in Santa's eyes said he felt caught between a rock and a hard place, but he suddenly nodded. "Yes, Christy."

"Deep sigh," she said, blowing out a long one and letting her shoulders sag with relief. Feeling as if the weight of the world had just been lifted from her shoulders, she skipped down the stairs from the stage, suddenly sure this would be the best Christmas ever. Oh, her parents would be mad when they realized she'd run away from home to meet Santa. But by Christmas, which meant tomorrow morning, her mom and dad would be in love again, and they'd realize Christy had simply had no choice.

Chapter One

Joy Holt couldn't have just gotten fired. Ted in the sales department, sure. He came late, left early and took three-hour lunches. Or Claire in art. For years, people swore she was about to get the ax.

But not Joy.

She'd thought her job as an editor was rock solid. She was never late to work, was a trendy dresser, and was always the very first employee on sign-up sheets for office parties. Why, everybody said it was a toss-up which was better—her Cajun meatballs, buffalo wings or guacamole—so Joy always went ahead and made all three. Everybody agreed she was, no question, the most reliable, hardest worker at Stern, Wylie and Morrow. A real cheerleader. A stand-up gal. Joy of Gibraltar, that's what they called her.

Saint Joy.

Some even used Ryan's old nickname for her, Joy-to-the-world.

Hadn't she held the fort when all the folks up on nine got food poisoning after accidentally ordering that bad sushi? And hadn't she personally ridden the train six hours a week, hand-delivering work to the publisher on the q.t. after that horseback riding accident upstate? There was nothing Joy wouldn't do for her boss! Besides, it was Christmas Eve, and even Stern, Wylie and Morrow—otherwise known as SWM because all the upper brass were, in fact single white males—wasn't *that* heartless.

Nevertheless, Joy was being escorted through the somber, dark-paneled hallways of the publishing house on Fifty-second and Madison where she'd spent the past six of her twenty-seven years, flanked by a black-suited security guard whose hand rested on the gun strapped to his hip, and a stern, matronly woman who'd been introduced as a "management-employee transitions liaison." *Whatever that means,* Joy thought now.

It just didn't seem real.

But then a lot of things in Joy's life didn't seem real lately. Her divorce from Ryan, for starters. Or that Joy and Ryan's baby girl, Christy, wasn't even a baby anymore, but was somehow managing to turn eight years old this Christmas. Or the fact that Joy's aunt May had died, and the teenager whom Ryan *thought* was Aunt May's daughter was coming to New York to live with Joy after the holidays.

But of course "Aunt May's daughter" was quite the little family secret...

Oh, Lord.

Joy's eyes widened. *Just don't go there. Don't even start thinking about all that, not yet, not right now.*

Still feeling stunned, Joy glanced to her left, catching a last glimpse of the office where she'd been buried under paperwork for the past few years of her life.

"My pictures," Joy suddenly said. "Pictures of my daughter are still on my bulletin board."

One of Ryan, too. Even after signing the divorce papers, Joy hadn't been able to take it down. The Polaroid had been shot on the rooftop garden of their apartment building, where Ryan was standing in front of the gas grill, taking a break from flipping burgers. Wearing a chef's apron that said Big Bad Dad, he'd thrust a spatula-free hand on his hip. His short dark hair was sticking endearingly up, and he was squinting against blowing wind, his dark eyes looking sad and serious. Joy knew he'd been gazing at the New York skyline, but every time she looked at him now, she'd think, *Ryan's remembering how in love we were, and it's making him sad.*

"The pictures," Joy said again, "I have to get the pictures of my daughter and husband." *Ex*-husband, Joy knew she should have said, but she still couldn't call him that, not even if they lived two thousand miles apart. Ryan could live in another galaxy, and he'd still remain her husband.

Sometimes now, late at night, Joy would shut her eyes and try to imagine a man other than Ryan lying beside her in bed. She'd concentrate so hard her head hurt...until she could finally feel the man's warm body, his naked skin, his firm dry palms gliding slowly over her. She'd keep telling herself that her dream-lover was big, brawny and blond, but it never worked. Every time Joy put a face to the hands, the eyes and hair would turn out to be dark brown, almost black—Ryan's. "I've missed you so much," he'd whisper. Now Joy blinked to dispel the image of him.

"Any belongings you've left here will be sent," the woman assured her. "Including your pictures."

"But—"

"Please, Ms. Holt," a security guard said, "we urge you to remain calm."

"Not to worry," Joy said, though she was feeling anything but calm. "I don't intend to go postal." Nor would she cry, she told herself when she felt her eyes tear. But she'd miss this place. And losing a job she'd held for years was just another indication to Joy that everything in her life—*in her and Ryan's lives*—had spun, and was still spinning, out of control.

To think, Joy had been so excited when she'd been called into Melinda Keen's office. She'd thought she was getting an extra Christmas bonus. Already, Joy had been thinking about buying Christy another Christmas present with the money.

A minute later, she'd found herself croaking,

"You're letting me go?" Pausing, she'd suddenly chuckled with relief. "Oh, of course, Melinda! You mean you're letting me go *early* because it's Christmas Eve."

But Melinda had slowly shaken her head. "We knew you'd understand," she'd begun diplomatically, looking unusually crisp in her red suit, the perfectly blunt-cut ends of her brunette bob just touching a pearl choker. "As you know, we've been holding out hope that you'd get Jon Sleet to write a book this year and boost Christmas sales. In the past, he's been such a moneymaker for SWM."

"I know all about Jon Sleet's success," Joy had managed to say. "I discovered him." It was hardly Joy's fault that family tragedy had touched the author's life and caused him to stop writing.

"We know," Melinda'd returned bluntly. "But..." Suddenly Melinda had blown out a short peeved sigh and leaned forward. "Look," she'd continued. "I probably shouldn't say even this, but in the current market, with sales down and SWM struggling to survive, we need to see more initiative. More big-bad attitude. More can-do."

More initiative? How many nights had Joy left this office after everyone else? How many times had she been running ragged with her own responsibilities, only to find herself helping Melinda with a special project? And all that time, Joy was under the gun, also needing to rush from the office to take Christy to a doctor's appointment, school play or dance lesson. Because, of course, Joy's husband couldn't be bothered. Ryan's job had always been so much more important than hers.

How could she have tried so hard to be a perfect wife, mother and employee—only to find herself divorced, unemployed and alone on Christmas?

Not at Christmas. The holiday was filled with memories, especially since Joy and Ryan's daughter had been born on Christmas morning. And as much as Joy fought it, she'd started remembering...

Ryan's soft dark eyes in the delivery room on Christmas morning eight years ago, when he'd first seen their baby girl.

The tiny Christmas tree he'd brought to the hospital.

The matching white lace nightgowns embroidered with holly leaves that he'd picked out for her and the baby.

But that was nearly eight years ago. And now Christy was visiting her daddy in L.A. for the holidays while Joy was alone. Soon, a daughter no one even knew Joy had was coming to live with her, too. Even thirteen-year-old Elayne thought Aunt May had been her mother, not Joy. The lies and betrayals were bad enough, but how was Joy going to raise two girls in New York City without a job?

But Melinda hadn't cared. She'd merely turned Joy over to the duo who now escorted her through the lobby doors to a waiting limo.

"Deep breath," she suddenly whispered, staring at the shiny black car that looked more like a hearse. Hugging her coat around her, she paused, simply breathing in the cold Manhattan air.

Whatever happens, Joy told herself firmly, *it'll all work out fine. I'll do anything for my kids. They're all that matter.*

As Joy took another deep breath, the management-employee transitions liaison slid a plastic binder under Joy's arm, saying, "SWM wishes you the very best of luck, Ms. Holt."

I'll bet. "Thanks," Joy said.

She got into the car, and the limo driver, who'd apparently already been given her address, pulled wordlessly from the curb. Only then did Joy stare down into her lap, and read the title on the plastic bindered booklet: How To Write Your Résumé.

She couldn't help but smile.

Turning, Joy stared back at the midtown skyscraper. Then, lifting a hand, she drew a heart with an arrow through it in the condensation of the back window, the way Ryan used to when they'd been huddled together, whispering intimately and getting warm in the back seats of cabs in winter. For a second, she pretended he was beside her, and her throat constricted. Right now, she needed him so much.

She needed him to hold her, the way he had in the early days of their marriage—because his was the only body that would ever feel right.

And she needed him to talk to—because Ryan's was the only advice she'd trust about her daughter, her other daughter, the one he didn't even know she'd had.

The daughter I now need to financially support.

Joy's heart skipped a beat. For the past eight months, Ryan had been sending generous checks for the maintenance of the West Side apartment they used to share, but with another child to care for…

Suddenly Joy straightened in the seat. When Jon Sleet stopped writing, SWM sent people to his hometown, to beg him to start working again. Joy had always refused to go because it was family tragedy that had made Jon stop. But now tragedy had touched Joy's family. Her husband was gone and she needed a job to support her daughters. If she could convince Jon Sleet to write again, she could get the SWM job back. It was a long shot, but…

Joy opened the partition between the seats. "When we get to the apartment, would you mind waiting? I want to grab a bag and make a second stop."

"You're going…?"

"To La Guardia Airport." *If you want initiative, Melinda, she thought, her mood lifting, get a load of this.*

But Joy's smile faltered as the driver rounded the corner of Fifty-ninth and Fifth because her gaze landed on Central Park and the wrought-iron lamp under which Ryan had proposed nearly nine years ago. She could still remember the strength in his body as he'd pulled her to him and how he'd looked, leaning against the low stone wall that stretched around Central Park, with the lamplight shining in his dark hair. They were in college then—her at NYU, him at Columbia—and the weather had been gray and cold, just like today. They'd been running for a cab they'd missed, and they'd both been breathless.

C'mon, Joy.

You're nuts.

No, I'm in love. And I want it in writing that you'll never leave me. Nothing else matters to me anymore.

Me, neither, Ryan.

Does that mean you'll marry me?

Yes, she'd managed to answer. And then she was suddenly laughing and crying at the same time. *Why not?* she'd said. *I mean…why not?*

Now, fresh tears gathered in Joy's eyes. Because she knew that all the initiative in the world could never bring Ryan back.

Christmas Eve, 12:00 p.m.
Los Angeles

"MY DAUGHTER IS *WHERE*?" Ryan Holt had been staring at the cloudy brown haze hanging over L.A. Gripping the portable phone, he now paced the deck that wrapped around his parents' stilted house on Manhattan Beach, then he stopped and leaned against the deck's railing, which was twined with

Christmas lights. "You're serious?" he asked. "You're saying Christy ran away?"

The man on the phone talked quickly—he'd identified himself as Sheriff Steve Warwick of Holiday Hamlet, North Carolina—and as he talked, Ryan's eyes continued assessing his surroundings with a calm he didn't begin to feel. He stared where the sun glanced off the ocean's cresting waves, then through the open sliding glass doors leading into his parents' living room. Inside the house, the Christmas tree lights, which were on a timer, suddenly snapped on.

While the sheriff explained the situation, Ryan's first impulse was to place blame. He wasn't proud of it...but damn Joy! Couldn't she even put their daughter safely on a plane? But really, Ryan knew this was all *his* fault. When Christy called, saying plans had changed and that he wasn't to pick her up at the airport until the day after Christmas, he'd believed her. Hell, Ryan would have believed anything if it meant not having to talk to his ex-wife.

Blowing out a sigh, he let his mind race: Why did his seven-year-old daughter lie all the time now? Why had she become so manipulative since the divorce? Why, whenever she wanted something, couldn't his little girl just ask directly?

Just how bad a father were you, Ryan?

Staring mutely under the Christmas tree, Ryan took in all the gifts with Christy's name on them. His mother, Maggie, was now rushing toward him, coming from the kitchen where she'd been cooking for tomorrow's Christmas dinner, still wiping her hands on a dish towel. "Ryan? Is everything all right with Christy?"

"Christy?" Ryan's father called, appearing worriedly from the den where he'd been watching TV. "What the heck's going on here, Ryan?"

Ryan quickly covered the phone's mouthpiece with his hand. "I think she's fine, I—" Uncovering the phone, he continued listening to Sheriff Warwick's assurances.

"It's really that simple," the sheriff was saying. "Your little girl's been in Holiday Hamlet for about a week. Near as we can tell, she was on her way to Los Angeles, to spend Christmas with you, but her plane got grounded here because of bad weather. Rather than stay at the airport, the way she was supposed to, she walked out and caught a cab up to Jon Sleet's house. He's an author of children's books who lives around here. Anyhow, I guess your daughter's a big fan..."

Of course she was. Every kid loved Jonathan Sleet's books. Ryan vaguely remembered a night, years ago, when he and Joy had entertained Jon in their Manhattan apartment. Ryan had liked the writer immensely, and it was with great sorrow that he'd later heard the man had lost his wife and child.

"My wife used to work with Jon Sleet," Ryan found himself saying. "She was his editor in New York."

But Christy had been gone a week? Ryan thought as the sheriff continued talking. Despite the repeated assurances that his daughter was safe, Ryan's chest continued tightening with tension and worry. Strangely the sensations made him feel as if he was back in the rat race, working in real estate in Manhattan again. Back then, he'd always felt edgy. He'd always felt he was about to lose a celebrity client, a multimillion dollar deal, a hot piece of Fifth Avenue property. But lose a—

Child?

"Christy," Ryan stated. "Is she at Jon's house now? Or is she there with you? Can I talk to her?"

"No, she's at Jon's. She's—"

"A *week?*" Ryan suddenly interrupted. He told himself to put a lid on it, but explosive emotions were in his nature. "How could she be gone a week? She's only *seven.* Joy—that's my wife, I mean, my ex-wife—"

"We know who she is," Sheriff Warwick interjected calmly. "We're still trying to locate her."

Another cause for concern. Ryan's fingers curled more tightly around the phone. "She works at Stern, Wylie and Morrow. It's a publishing house in Manhattan."

"We tried there, but they've let their employees go early."

"Doesn't matter." Knowing Joy—or rather, knowing her boss Melinda—Joy would still be chained to her desk. "Believe me, she's probably there but not answering the phone. She lives in that office."

"Well, we'll keep trying to find her."

"You're *sure* my wife's not there with Christy?" Ryan flinched, correcting himself again. "*Ex*-wife."

"No. Your daughter definitely came alone."

Somehow, it still wouldn't sink in. "But Christy said she wasn't going to fly out until the day after Christmas. I..." Fear curled inside him. Had his little girl *really* run away? Was she *that* unhappy? While Ryan forced himself not to imagine the countless horrible things that could have happened to his daughter, any further protests died on his lips. He listened mutely, just getting all the facts. Finally he said, "I'll be on the next flight out."

"You're leaving?" Maggie said as he hung up.

Ryan nodded and explained the situation, repeating the sheriff's words as if that might make everything make sense.

"She wouldn't even tell the sheriff her full name, or where she lived," Ryan concluded. "Or who her parents were."

His father said, "Your mother and I'd better come with you."

"No, Pop. I appreciate it, but—"

"Well then, son, you'd best hurry and get packing. I'll book your flight."

"Thanks, Pop."

Ryan took off, heading for his childhood bedroom, which he'd been using since the divorce. "Ma," he said to Maggie who was on his heels, guilt choking his voice, "I knew something was wrong when Christy called and said we weren't supposed to pick her up at the airport for another week.''

"That child," Maggie said simply, her voice holding both love and censure for her first grandbaby. "If there's hot water to sink neck-deep into, she'll dive. I swear, she was born going on thirty."

Unsuccessfully trying to tamp down his temper, Ryan allowed himself one murderous sigh. "From what Sheriff Warwick said, it sounds as if she's having herself a dandy time." He shrugged, opening drawers and assessing what to take.

"I knew you should have talked to Joy when Christy called. Oh, why didn't you, Ryan?"

Because the sound of his wife's voice broke his heart. His mother knew it, too. He shot her a look as if to say so, but Maggie was busy, tugging a rolling Pullman from under the bed.

"Here, Ma." Taking over, Ryan put the suitcase on top of the bed. As he lifted folded stacks of clothes from the drawers, Maggie anxiously repeated phrases she'd overheard from his phone conversation. "So, she really got off a plane all by herself...and then took a cab?"

"She lives in New York," Ryan stated with far more assurance than he felt. "She's used to getting cabs. And the sheriff says she's fine." Dangerously smart for her age, too, Ryan silently added. And, since the divorce, obviously confused.

"My poor, poor grandbaby," Maggie sighed. "Are you sure your dad and I shouldn't come?"

"No. You stay." Ryan glanced up, his gaze softening. First thing tomorrow, his four siblings and their spouses and kids would descend. All day, Maggie had been in the kitchen, cooking up the Holt family's favorite dishes, which she always served for the holiday meal. "You and Pop have a good Christmas with the family."

For a minute, Ryan and his mother just stood there—gazes touching, hearts linked and aching. Both were thinking of Christmases past, when Ryan, Joy and Christy had been here together...a family. Ryan could almost hear the laughter and squeals as Christy and the other kids ripped crinkling wrapping paper from their presents.

He also remembered Joy's strange silences that he'd never understood. Oh, Joy made a big deal out of Christmas, especially since it was also Christy's birthday. But Ryan would always find Joy alone at some point in the day—staring sadly at the ocean from the deck, or at the street from the bedroom window. And at those moments, the unreachably distant look in her eyes would fill him with unbearable pain. Silently Ryan would watch without her knowing, hating that there were parts of his wife's inner life that he would never touch, never understand, never share. Her secrecy had hurt him so much, not that he'd known how to approach her.

Each time he'd seen her like that, he'd wanted to grip her shoulders hard, and beg, *Joy, don't shut me out. Please, baby, let me in.* But he couldn't bring himself to be so vulnerable, so instead, for what seemed a thousand times, Ryan had only casually asked her what she was thinking.

A thousand times, Joy had just as casually answered, "Nothing."

Now, Maggie was squeezing a waffle-knit thermal shirt into his bag. "It'll be cold there and you'll need it. And, Ryan, maybe you should take some of Christy's presents. Will you be bringing her back here for the rest of the holiday?"

Ryan knew his mother had her heart set on seeing her first grandchild this Christmas. There were eight more grandkids now, but Christy would always be the first...special. "I don't know, Ma. I'll try." When he looked up, his mother was surveying him with kind, liquid eyes.

"I know what you think," she said, her voice gentle. "But you're wrong, honey. You're a good father."

"Thanks," he said. "But I wasn't."

"You are now," his mother conceded.

God, he wanted to be. Ever since he walked out of his and Joy's apartment eight months ago, he tried to change. Nowadays, he was doing things with his life that Joy wouldn't even believe. Not that he'd tell her.

As he circled the bed, his mother's hand stayed him. "Maybe when you get there, you'll see Joy," she said. "Maybe you'll..."

Get back together.

He tilted his head, his smile wry. "We're divorced."

"But you love her."

He shrugged. "I left." He started to look away, but his mother's eyes firmly held his. God love her. Maggie Holt believed in three things—the liberal use of garlic as a curative, the healing power of her homemade chicken soup and true love. She believed there was only one man for one woman, and that those two halves made a whole so strong that nothing could ever divide it. When you got married, she believed, it was always for keeps.

Ryan and Joy Holt had once believed that, too.

"But you love her," Maggie said again.

"Yeah," Ryan admitted on a sigh. "Yeah, Ma, I do." How could a man stop loving a woman he'd slept with for eight, nearly nine, years? A woman with whom he'd started a family?

Suddenly his mother smiled, patting his arm. "Well, then, I bet you'll be surprised by this trip."

Ryan's lips parted, but he said nothing. Twenty-eight years of being Maggie Holt's son told him protest was useless. She'd never believe his and Joy's marriage was over, especially not when he and Joy shared a child.

As he lifted the suitcase from the bed, Ryan's mind filled with images of Christy. She was a beautiful kid, with Joy's emerald eyes and wispy, wavy white-blond hair that felt as soft as shredded cotton. In his mind's eye, he saw Christy as she was years ago, crawling with the speed of lightning, sinking her chubby fingers and toes into the curly pile of the living room carpet in New York.

"There's pace for you," he'd laughed.

"Definitely a born New Yorker," Joy had said, chuckling.

For the past eight months, he'd been talking to Christy on the phone at least once a week. They talked for hours, too. Hell, he talked to his daughter more now than when they'd lived under the same roof. And she amused him as she always had, especially when she announced she was going to travel when she grew up, and started practicing her languages on him.

"Bonjour, Papa!" she'd venture in a ridiculous French accent. And when they signed off, it was always, *"Au revoir"* or *"ciao."*

God, he loved her. And yet he hadn't seen her for eight months.

Eight months!

It was too long to go without hugging his daughter, without smelling her little-kid scent or seeing her impish, mischievous grin.

His mother hadn't given up. "Joy still loves you, too, Ryan."

Ryan's gaze caught hers and he cracked a slow, wry smile. "You're hopeless. You know that, Ma?"

She smiled back, her dark eyes looking strangely smug. "Hmm. We'll see who's hopeless, Ryan."

TOYING WITH THE DIAL on the broken radio of the last rental car that had been available at the airport, Ryan squinted through the windshield, watching the thumping wipers push snow from one side to the other. Despite the urge to punch the gas, he drove slowly, since the roads were icy. The wonders of modern technology, he thought. In six hours, he'd made it all the way to the other side of the country. Day had given way to night, heat to zero-degree temperatures, and sunshine to snow.

Giving into his impulses, Ryan had finally called Joy from the plane, but she wasn't home or at the office.

What if his wife had a *date?*

Tightening his hands on the steering wheel, Ryan suddenly imagined romantic firelight flickering on Joy's skin, two round warm goblets of brandy clinking together and a sexy sophisticated guy who happened to look a lot like George Clooney tilting back his head to better hear Joy's soft laughter and her husky whisper.

Ryan's throat got tight. What if they were *naked?*

Reaching, he rubbed a clear patch in the condensation of the windshield. *We're divorced,* he tried to reason. Besides, what was good for the goose was good for the gander. After all, *he'd* dated since the divorce.

"Yeah, right, Ryan," he muttered. "Once."

She'd been nice, too…so nice that she'd kindly patted his back all night, nodding with maternal sympathy while he talked about Joy. *Get over it, Ryan. Your wife—ex-wife—is an attractive, single woman alone on Christmas. As far as she knows, her daughter's with her daddy. Why shouldn't she go out?*

Because...well, Joy just *shouldn't,* that's why.

As Ryan continued cruising through Holiday Hamlet, the night seemed colder, darker and snowier. It was hard to believe it was still eighty degrees in L.A. When the inn where his father had booked a room came into sight, Ryan concentrated doubly hard, since the mountain road leading to it was so slick.

Enough snow had fallen that he knew he wasn't going to see Christy tonight. He'd already been to Jon Sleet's. When no one answered the door, Ryan had called the inn from a pay phone in town—only to find out that Jon had just left. The deputy who had come to the phone said Jon and Ryan had probably passed each other on the road, and that he didn't know if Joy had been reached. At this point, he said, Ryan should get a good night's sleep at the inn, then head for Jon's in the morning, when the roads were clear.

But was Joy in Holiday Hamlet or not?

All during the flight, Ryan had replayed scenes from their marriage. He'd cursed himself, too, for never looking deep enough into Joy's character to realize how rarely she voiced her desires. Why hadn't he noticed how seldom she said what she wanted from him, what she needed?

All those years, he'd been such a taker.

And Joy gave and gave.

Over and over, on the plane, he'd relived that

moment eight months ago, when he'd been offered a cushy real estate job in L.A. He'd found Joy on their fenced-in roof, watching Christy play on the jungle gym.

"So, you're moving to L.A.," Joy had said when he told her. "Good for you."

Until that moment, Ryan had never even considered taking the job. He'd just been proud that a prestigious company had offered it. Perversely, he'd said, "So, I guess you're not coming, huh?"

"I didn't hear you ask."

By then, they'd been so estranged that Ryan had countered by actually taking the job. Within a month, Joy had sent divorce papers to L.A. Feeling strangely railroaded, Ryan had signed.

Now he pulled into a parking space at the inn, his eyes searching the upper windows, half hoping Joy would be staring down...waiting for him.

She wasn't.

The place was charming, though—a three-story stone cottage with outbuildings and sloping snow-blanketed grounds. Getting out and grabbing the suitcase, Ryan ran through slush with his city shoes, suddenly glad his mother had insisted he pack hiking boots.

"Ryan Holt," he said at the front desk, introducing himself. "Is my...my *wife* here? Joy Holt?"

"Dang it all," the sixtyish man behind the scarred but polished desk said with a twangy mountain accent, "you would ask the one thing I ain't able to answer." He thrust a harried hand through his bushy gray hair, and thoughtfully tongued a chipped front tooth. "Sorry, Mr. Holt," he added, "but I done took over desk duty from the wife, so I'll have to ask her about Mrs. Holt. Meantime, should I give you a separate room?"

Ryan was now hard-pressed to explain that he and Joy would need separate rooms, anyway. *If she comes.* "Please."

Frowning as the man took his cash deposit, Ryan realized this was an informal establishment. No registration book was in sight. Glancing through an archway, he could see that the costume party his daughter had attended earlier was still in full swing. For a heartbeat, he thought he saw Joy, dressed as an ornamental ball.

His breath caught, but it wasn't her. And then, for a fiercely painful moment, he could almost feel her slender body crushed hard against him. Remembering her embraces made his whole body hurt with a cold, frozen longing to soak up the heat he'd been missing from hers.

In reality, they'd probably shake hands if they met.

Trying to push Joy from his thoughts, Ryan said, "Christmas costume party?"

"Tradition 'round these parts." The man untangled a thumb that was hooked around the strap of his bib overalls, then thrust out a hand. "Name's Hub Scudder. Me 'n my wife, Pam, run this here place."

Ryan glanced around appreciatively. "Nice."

"Lotsa history here, but we been lookin' to sell and retire. Fact is, Sheriff Warwick said you were a big-city real estate guy and I was thinkin'—"

"The sheriff told you I was in real estate?"

Hub shrugged. "Small town," he explained. "Word gets around quick. Met your little girl, a'course. Cute as a button. Though for seven years old, I gotta say she's a handful."

"Well, she's eight tomorrow," Ryan offered dryly, not feeling nearly as unconcerned as his tone might have indicated.

"That so?" Hub chuckled. "Guess that explains it. But you'd better watch her, 'cause she's a travelin' kind of gal. Earlier, she done counted to ten for me in four different languages."

Ryan couldn't help but smile. "I warn you," he said. "She gets real mad if you ask her about anything between eleven and twenty."

"I'll remember that," Hub said with another chuckle as he circled the desk on spindly legs, then motioned Ryan toward the stairs. "Too bad you missed Santa Claus," he continued conversationally. "The kids, including yours, got plumb tuckered out and went home, too. But there's still youngsters in from college, some old folks and singles. The wife laid out a costume for you, in case you'd like to come down for some victuals."

Ryan smiled. "No costume for you, huh?"

"Wouldn't be caught dead all dressed up at sixty-six." He chuckled. "Anyway, what say? You wouldn't want to buy yourself an old inn, would you?''

A year ago Ryan would have. Of course, a year ago, he'd also have bulldozed the place and built a strip mall. Not that he'd tell Hub Scudder that.

Hub swung open the door to Ryan's room. ''Home sweet home, Mr. Holt.''

''Thanks.'' Ryan took in the fire crackling in the fireplace, and the warm country appointments. On top of the bright quilted bed was a Santa suit.

''It's all Pam could round up,'' Hub explained. ''Hope the dang thing fits.''

Ryan was tempted to forget the weather and drive to Jon Sleet's. Even if Christy was asleep, he wanted to hug her tight. He wanted to wake her up and make sure she understood how much her daddy loved her.

Why did you run away, baby?

Ryan swallowed hard. Well, if he sat up here alone, he'd definitely just keep thinking about Joy and Christy—and the mess of their lives.

''Santa Claus, huh?'' Ryan said, parking his suitcase beside the bed. ''Sounds good to me.''

Chapter Two

"Live a little, darlin'. Or are you too lost in thought to help yourself to another drink?"

Joy glanced up from a love seat in front of the fire, into the eyes of a middle-aged man who was dressed as an elf, in head-to-toe green. She'd been mulling over a magazine article she'd read during the flight from New York that said eighty-five percent of married people polled kept a secret from their spouse that would destroy the marriage.

Eighty-five percent!

Had Ryan withheld a secret? Or was Joy the only one?

"Well," she conceded, lifting a mug of something hot, buttery and spiked with dark rum from the elf's tray. "I guess I'm not going anywhere tonight. Not in this snow. Why *not* have another?"

Why not? Because you haven't had so much as one for almost fourteen years, not since the night when…when…

Joy closed her eyes.

When she opened them, she was staring into the

gray stone fireplace and roaring, mesmerizing fire. Forked tongues of flame were licking around heavy logs and, over the hum of Christmas music and chatter, she could hear the fire spit. Along with scents from the food table Joy could smell burning sap, a scent as sweet as the rum-spiked drink warming her travel-tired bones. Vaguely she realized she was on her third toddy, which meant she'd already had three too many. Her whole body, like the fire, was turning warm.

Or maybe it was just the costume.

When Joy arrived, the inn's proprietress, Pam Scudder, had offered her a Mrs. Claus costume. "Now, honey child," Pam had said, as Joy stared at the granny glasses and white wig that was twirled into a matronly bun, "why don't you join our little party and get yourself some victuals?"

Victuals.

Joy had chuckled softly at how the quaint word made New York City seem continents away. There wasn't even a single city light here.

Had SWM really fired her today? Right now, relaxing before a fire, Joy's limo ride down Madison Avenue seemed like a dream, as did the flight to North Carolina and the snowy, hour-long drive from the airport to the inn.

Did she even *want* her job back?

Did she even *want* to live in New York City?

At the questions that threatened everything she held dear, Joy's heart squeezed. *Oh, don't be ridiculous! Of course I want those things!* Unfortunately it was Christmas Eve and too late to talk to Jon Sleet about his publishing career.

Glancing from the fireplace, she looked around. She'd made obligatory small talk with the party-goers, of course, but her heart wasn't in it. Not when the holiday atmosphere kept reminding her, somehow, of Christmases with Christy and Ryan.

Eighty-five percent, she thought again as party-goers swirled around her in a blur of red, green and gold, their voices merging with the Christmas music. Would divulging her secret have destroyed her marriage? Did it even matter anymore, since she and Ryan were divorced? Another log snapped and fell into the embers, sending a spray of red sparks whooshing up the chimney, and then, still watching the entrancing flames, Joy started seeing images from the past...

She remembered being fifteen, back in Aunt May's kitchen in Beckley, West Virginia. She'd been gabbing on the phone about the new cheer-leading uniforms they'd gotten at school, when an official voice beeped in, asking for Mrs. or Mr. Jerald Jones. Seconds later, Aunt May's lips had twisted into an anguished frown as she got the news. Pressing her hand to her heart, she'd listened carefully while the man told her Joy's parents had died in an accident outside Parkersburg.

Joy also remembered her mother, primping in the bedroom, getting ready for that trip. Sunday clothes were strewn across the bed as she packed. "Joy, which handbag?" her mother had asked fretfully, holding two against her suit. "Be honest." She was accompanying Joy's dad on a business trip, and she wanted to make a good impression, the best.

Of course no one on earth would ever know that, after an hour's deliberation, Joy and her mom had decided on a green drawstring bag. The decision had seemed so crucial at the time, but later, recalling it, only filled Joy with a sense of futility since her mother had never had a chance to carry the bag.

Maybe it was that sense of futility that drove her into the arms of a boy who was too old for her during a school dance. Feeling bold, she'd cozied up to some of the wilder kids and tried some moonshine. And then some more. For the first time, family tragedy had slipped from her mind. Slipped further away still when she'd found herself in a deserted classroom, letting Doug Ritts's kisses sweep away the past. She'd barely known what was happening when he pushed up her skirt, let down his pants and then surged inside her.

Only when the spring term was over did Joy confess the pregnancy she'd hidden under loose clothes for months. "You just turned sixteen," Aunt May and Uncle Jer had whispered, looking stricken.

And then came the saving grace. A scholarship Joy had applied for the previous autumn came through, and in addition to it, Joy could live with a family in Paris as an exchange student during her sophomore year.

Events snowballed after that. Until Elayne was born, Joy had stayed with a friend of Aunt May's who lived out of town, then Joy left for Paris. May and Jer, who'd had trouble conceiving and had considered adopting, took the baby to raise. Those few who suspected a formal adoption hadn't just come through kept it to themselves. After all, the Joneses were respected, and Joy was still a good girl, a scholarship student. The kind of girl who did Beckley proud.

It wasn't an ideal situation, but it was a solution. Joy would be able to see Elayne anytime she wanted. So what, if Elayne called her *Aunt* Joy, not mama?

But now everything had changed.

Uncle Jer had died years ago, but now Aunt May was gone, too, which meant ''Aunt Joy'' was thirteen-year-old Elayne's nearest relative. Not that Joy was close to her daughter. As much as she'd wanted to know her, the pain of seeing Elayne had turned out to be too great.

''She cries every time I hold her,'' Joy had nervously protested the first time she'd come back from Paris.

''I guess she's gotten used to me,'' Aunt May had explained.

Blinking back tears, Joy had drawn the shaking, crying bundle closer, but Elayne kept wailing, wanting to be held by someone else.

Anybody but me, Joy had thought. It was as if Elayne knew Joy had betrayed her. Elayne couldn't know Joy was really her mother, since she was only a baby, but it felt that way. Still only sixteen, Joy had fled back to Paris and extended the arrangements to live abroad. After that, no matter how much her aunt and uncle begged, Joy rarely returned, because when she did, seeing what was left of her family broke her heart.

"Auntie," three-year-old Elayne had pronounced one Christmas.

"That's right," Aunt May crooned. "Auntie Joy."

Somehow, Joy had hidden her tears and smiled, telling herself what the adults had—that it was all for the best. But it wasn't. At least not until Ryan Holt sauntered into Joy's life—filling her heart with love again and giving her another baby girl—one she could publicly claim as her own. Anytime Joy found herself dwelling on Elayne, she'd quickly remind herself that if she hadn't given her up, she'd have settled down in Beckley, West Virginia, and never have met Ryan. As it was, Joy had left Paris for a second scholarship, this one to college in New York.

Now a grown woman, Joy stared into the mesmerizing fire, and for the second time in her life, she felt the warmth of alcohol pulse through her veins. How had she lost Ryan, Elayne, her job? How had she wound up alone on Christmas?

"Hey." The voice was soft. "What're you thinking?"

Maybe because of the drinks, maybe because her mind was still a million miles away, maybe because being alone on Christmas was so damnably depressing, Joy kept her eyes on the fire a second, not even looking up at the elf waiter when she answered, "Mostly my daughter and husband." She corrected herself. "Ex-husband."

"Ex-husband?"

Smiling ruefully, she slowly began raising her gaze. "Some days I'm afraid I still love him." The comment was offhand, dryly delivered. But now her heart suddenly stuttered because Joy realized that the man towering over her and staring down into her eyes was, indeed, Ryan Holt.

Ryan!

"Oh, no," she whispered. "I thought you were the elf."

Ryan squinted. "The elf?"

It was hardly what Joy had expected Ryan to say, if they ever saw each other again. Still in shock, she said, "The elf who brought the drinks." She hadn't moved except to tighten her grip around the mug handle.

For a minute, they kept staring, awkwardly unsure of what to say next. *Let him talk.*

Gripping the mug even more tightly, Joy started to ask him if he'd like to sit down, but she couldn't get her mouth around the words. And this ridiculous Mrs. Claus costume! Her new haircut was obscured by a matronly wig, and even though she'd lost ten pounds, the padded costume hid it. When she saw Ryan again, if ever, Joy had wanted to look great, to shoot him her best devil-may-care grin, as if she'd thrown caution to the wind and was having the time of her life.

Instead they were dressed as a couple—Mr. and Mrs. Claus. Unbelievable coincidence, she thought as her muzzy head started reeling. Wait a minute! Was Pam Scudder playing matchmaker?

And anyway, Joy suddenly wondered, what was Ryan doing here? Where was Christy? Setting aside the drink mug, Joy suddenly hoped Ryan would notice she'd quit biting her nails. A second later, she hoped not, since if he did, he'd also notice how badly her hands were shaking. She clasped them together. "Ryan?"

Her tone demanded an explanation for his presence.

His lips parted—at least what she could see of them between the white Santa beard and mustache—and she suddenly feared what he was about to say. The past eight months, during which they'd spoken only through lawyers and Christy, hung between them like a black curtain. Had she really just told her ex-husband she feared she still loved him? It was the truth, but she'd definitely rather he not know.

"Hey, Joy," he ventured.

"You can't get much more cautious than that opener," she returned dryly, managing to offer him a small, tight smile.

He actually chuckled, if warily. "Do I need to play it safe here?"

"It's Christmas," she returned, glad that damnable warble had left her voice. "I won't create a scene." Actually it was Ryan, not her, who was the scene-maker.

"I'm fresh out of scenes, myself."

She doubted it. Ryan could always fly off the handle. But what did he want? Why was he here? Had he come here searching for her...to make up?

He must have! She could think of no other possible explanation for meeting him at an inn in the middle of nowhere. Ryan was a hotshot, wheeling-dealing L.A. real estate agent. He definitely had better things to do than spend Christmas Eve in a backwoods mountain town. During their marriage, Joy couldn't have dragged him, kicking and screaming, to a place such as this. Which meant he must have called and her gotten her travel information from the concierge in their old building. Christy must be upstairs, asleep in one of the inn's rooms....

Ryan wants us to spend Christmas together!

Now it seemed so obvious, evident from the penetrating intensity of his dark-eyed gaze. Feeling a rush of nervousness, Joy managed to stand, smoothing her ridiculous costume and telling herself not to reveal too many of her feelings yet, not until he shared his. *If* he shared his. He rarely had during their marriage, at least not at the end. "Good to see you, Ryan." And it was. No matter how hard she tried, she couldn't stop her gaze from slipping over him. God, she'd missed him.

When she lifted her eyes, she was surprised to find him looking vulnerable. Ryan Holt...looking vulnerable? she thought with shock. Oh, maybe he had in the early years, before he'd turned into the kind of hard-nosed businessman who started his day by simultaneously jogging in Central Park and screaming orders into a cell phone, then showering by six-thirty a.m.

The sudden catch in his voice was even more jarring than the naked emotion in his gaze. "You miss me, Joy? You really think you might still love me?"

She squinted at him a long moment, her eyes flickering from the furry white ball at the tip of his Santa cap, down to his velvet shirt and baggy pants. Squinting into his eyes again and self-consciously wondering if she was slightly slurring her words, she said, "Are you okay?"

He stared. "Sure, why?"

"This just isn't like you."

"I'm afraid I don't understand, Joy."

"Well, I don't feel like I'm talking to Ryan Holt. I mean, the one I married. What is it with the…"

"The…?"

Emotions. Soulful gazes. These lovesick big brown puppy-dog eyes, and the gentle, mournful tone of affection and concern. *Yes,* Joy thought, the rum making her mind fuzzy, there's something very definitely wrong here. She squinted harder. "Shouldn't you be working?" she said warily. "You know, leveling some houses to make a strip mall or something? Maybe dicing up some virgin oceanfront for a Red Roof Inn?"

Ryan had the nerve to look appalled. "On Christmas?"

Last Christmas, after they'd had dinner with his family in Manhattan Beach, Ryan had gone to a closing for a multimillion dollar high-rise in La Jolla. "Yes," Joy said levelly. "On Christmas."

He ignored her tone. "I miss you," he ventured again.

She missed him, too, so much it hurt. Somehow, she managed a shrug as if to say *we're divorced,* and then she wished she hadn't wound up standing so close to him, since she could smell the arousing scent of his skin. He was wearing a Thierry Mugler cologne called Angel Men that Joy had first gotten at Bloomingdale's as a promotional sample. Advertised as having a roasted coffee aroma combined with the wooded outdoors, the scent had become something far more maddening on her husband. Blushing, Joy had pronounced it, "Bottled Hard Male," which had made Ryan laugh. Especially when she returned from the store the very next day, having purchased a full bottle. Ryan had been wearing the cologne for her ever since.

"Does it matter if I've missed you?" she finally said.

He nodded, looking strangely grave. "Yeah, I'm beginning to think it does."

"Why?" *Why are you here, Ryan? Did you really come to see me?*

His eyes flickered over her face, and her skin warmed as he took in each of her features—her green eyes, straight nose, the hint of dimples beside her small mouth. Even the way he was gazing at her gave her a start. He was staring as if he'd never seen her before—or never would again.

"It matters because I miss you, too. I—" Lifting a hand, Ryan traced where a stray silver-white wisp had fallen from her foolish wig and curled on her cheek. "Every day I miss the way it used to be."

Her insides were shaking like jelly. *Oh, no, you don't, Ryan Holt,* she thought. Damn him! "Don't you remember how estranged we became? Have you forgotten all those painful, long silences? How we stayed in different rooms in the apartment, avoiding each other like the plague?"

"Okay," he conceded. "Maybe I don't miss *everything* about the way things used to be."

"Good." Besides, touchy-feely conversation wasn't the sort a woman was supposed to have with the man she'd divorced. Nevertheless, Joy's heart suddenly wrenched, and she found herself softly adding, "Sorry, Ryan, but things *aren't* the way they used to be, are they?"

"Maybe not...but I still think about you all the time." Glancing away, Ryan released a rueful chuckle. "I think my mother knew when I saw you I'd..."

Despite common sense, the pulse in Joy's throat suddenly leaped with hope for reconciliation. She barely trusted her voice. "You'd?"

He shrugged. "Come right out and tell you how I felt."

She blew out a shaky breath. "That you miss me?"

"Yeah."

"Oh, Ryan," Joy sighed with a mournful catch in her voice.

He shook his head. "I know, Joy. Can you believe any of this? What have we done?"

And then, even though they knew a marriage between them could never work, he stepped forward just as she did, and they were in each other's arms.

RYAN DIDN'T RISK breathing. Holding Joy as close as he could, given the silly padded costumes, he was unable to believe it was even happening. Maybe his mother was right. Maybe this was his last chance with Joy. She lived in New York now. He lived in L.A. After this, maybe he'd never even see her again.

"I've wanted to hold you like this so bad," he confessed.

Her voice was small. "Okay, I admit it. Me, too."

"Then hold me, baby." Pulling her closer, oblivious to the thinning crowd of party-goers, Ryan slid his palms down, over the velvet back of her costume. As his fingers probed the ridges of her spine, remembering each bump, each groove, her face curved to the hollow of his neck. He felt where her forehead was warm from the fire, and he dragged in a deep pull of the perfume he'd always given her at Christmas.

"Chanel!" she'd exclaim every year. "Oh, you shouldn't have. It costs a fortune."

He'd always smile. "You're worth it." And she was.

From beneath the delicately musky perfume, Ryan now drew in scents of his wife, of what could never be bottled or bought and sold. "I didn't know what would happen if...if we ever saw each other again," he murmured.

"I thought we might shake hands," she whispered.

"I imagined that, too." Now the idea seemed ludicrous. Shake hands with Joy? Shake hands with a woman whose bed he'd shared for eight years? His voice turned husky. "I'm glad we can do this."

Except even he knew this was no friendly hug of greeting. Just her scent was arousing him, relentlessly pulling him in ways he couldn't deny, making him hard with want. She'd probably noticed his lack of control, but he didn't apologize. She'd been his *wife*. After over eight years of shared loving, a man would be dead if he didn't respond. Tightening his hands on her back, so she'd know he wasn't about to release her, he leaned inches back. His chest felt too tight, his breath too shallow. "You look good, Joy." As his eyes skimmed down her, the throaty catches in his lowered voice made clear how she was affecting him. "Real good."

She swallowed hard, but was unable to clear her voice. It came out husky. "You, too, Ryan."

"I—"

"I—"

Embarrassed color touched her pale cheeks and she chuckled when they began speaking at the same time. He said, "Should we make a wish?"

Her voice was unsteady. "You make it for both of us."

He stared into her eyes—the same slashes of winking, crystal emerald she'd given their daughter. How had he ever thought that the love between him and Joy was gone? *I wish we could get back together.*

He was sure she knew what he was thinking, and he offered a wry smile, his eyes narrowing as the corners of his mouth lifted. "Wishing never hurts," he whispered. Before she could respond, he felt a sudden tug of concern. "You've...lost some weight." He could see how prominent the bones of her face had become. "Are you okay?"

She blushed. "Okay, I admit it. I...got a little depressed after you left."

He wasn't sure what to say. "Sorry."

"It's okay."

But it wasn't. Nothing had been okay for a long time. He wanted her back. But this time, things would have to be different.

His eyes flickered over her face again, and he wondered if her hair was the same under the wig. It was usually so chic, dyed white-blond, with a hint of her honied roots showing, and cut short over her ears. Not many woman could get away with a style such as that, but Joy could.

Her hands flexed, pressing down on his shoulders. "What about Christy? Is she—"

Lifting a finger, Ryan silenced her with a touch to her lips. He'd had no earthly idea how he'd react to seeing her. But now he knew. His heart was aching to erase the part of their marriage when things had fallen apart. His body was yearning to possess her. Maggie Holt had been right, as mother's usually were. Ryan was still hopelessly in love. "Tonight, let's not talk about…" *Christy. The divorce.* Ryan figured Joy had been as worried as he when Sheriff Warwick finally tracked her down. "We're here right now, Joy. Maybe that's all that matters. And tomorrow…" *We'll pick up Christy.*

"Tomorrow's Christmas," Joy murmured. "And Christy's birthday."

Their gazes touched, and he was surprised to see that hers held none of the anger he expected. Instead they were slightly unfocused. A hint of a smile played on her lips, as if she was remembering all the good times, maybe the birth of their daughter.

Barely able to tear his eyes away, Ryan looked around, just long enough to see that no one was giving them a second glance. His eyes narrowed again. "Rum?" He only now registered that the scent was coming from Joy because in all the years of their marriage, he'd never once seen his wife drink. "You don't drink," he said. "Ever."

Her chin tilted up a notch. "You don't know everything about me, Ryan."

Something in her tone made his eyes narrow. "Maybe not." As his gaze settled on her lips, he decided the gentle curve of it was full of seductive promise.

She drew in a sharp breath. "But you do know some things," she conceded.

"I sure do." Before she could protest a kiss they both knew better than to indulge in, Ryan's mouth slanted across hers with probing heat and took the pleasure.

The way it used to be.

As his lips brushed hers, he remembered sharing cotton candy at Coney Island nine years ago...remembered how his heart raced when he kissed her that first time, locking his lips to hers as the roller coaster dropped down and little kids behind them screamed. Months later, he'd managed to slide his hands—both hands at once—into her panties and pull them down. Panting with arousal, he'd touched her sweet heat with embarrassingly unsteady caresses that still worked their magic since she'd let him...asked him...hell, begged him, to go all the way.

The way it used to be.

Oh, he knew better than to kiss her now, after all that had happened, but it was too late to stop. The old fire was there, and now the embers stirred as he dipped his tongue. When she dipped back, and the tips of their tongues touched, a pulse passed between them, making Ryan's heart wrench. Lord, what were they doing? *Needing, wanting, kissing.*

But they were divorced! Still, not even that could stop the heat that flooded his groin, or the weight of desire that began pulling him down...dragging his mouth harder and wetter on to Joy's. He felt himself sink even more. Down until he was drowning. Going deeper. Down...

The way it used to be.

EVERYTHING GOING THROUGH Joy's head as she kissed Ryan was sheer lunacy. She wanted him to move back home. Okay, sure it had been awful at the end, she was thinking, but maybe she could handle it now. Maybe everything would be different this time. Maybe they'd just needed a little breather, that's all. Didn't most couples need a little respite every once in a while? Besides, their daughter needed her daddy to come home.

Heat had risen on Joy's skin and in her blood. The kind of heat that made her forget her husband had become a kill-the-rainforest kind of Realtor. Or that she'd never told him everything about herself, that he didn't know her, not really. If he knew she'd given up a baby, he might not even *like* her. And anyway, she wondered, how would Ryan feel about being a father figure to Elayne?

We're not getting back together!

Pulling away an inch, she could still feel Ryan's uneven breath on her lips. He was aroused, and feeling the evidence of his need made her jittery. Desire had made his eyes darker, too, his hold on her tighter—and now she suddenly decided that

Ryan Holt just wasn't meant to be a Santa Claus. It wasn't so much that the velvet costume pants were too long, or that the white hair and beard didn't suit his coloring. But Santa's eyes were supposed to be blue and twinkling, not dark, devastating and deadly serious with sexual intent.

Her voice wasn't supposed to be this raspy, either. "We're *divorced*," she murmured, then glanced around, half expecting someone in the crowd to rub one index finger over the other, as if to say, "Shame." Of course, no one was paying them the least bit of attention.

As usual, Ryan got right to the point, his voice low and coaxing. "At the moment, I don't care if we're divorced."

Stated like a man.

But then, at the moment, she didn't care, either.

Let's go to bed.

She knew he was thinking it, too. She suddenly wanted to tear his clothes right off him. Oh, it was crass. But anyone who'd had a steady partner for years would understand, especially if they'd been alone for eight torturous months. And Ryan knew just exactly how to touch her...and it was so romantic in front of this fire on Christmas Eve...and his eyes were steaming, smoldering with dark heat that said he wanted it enough to simply take. Heaven help her, she really did, too.

Somehow, she forced herself to drop her hands, telling herself that she was going to walk away before it was too late, but then Ryan caught her fin-

gers and threaded his through hers. It made her remember how they used to twine hands while
making love. Ryan would get so wound up and excited that he'd growl and push her hands above her
head while his damp, hot body completely covered
hers.

His voice was low, slightly strained. "Feel it,
Joy?"

Sure do.

Need was sparking between them, pulsing
through her, making her lips and fingers tingle and
making her moist for what he so obviously intended
to give. She shouldn't have, but she'd dreamed of
this. She'd craved sex with Ryan. Swallowing hard,
she wondered if she could will away the bad memories of the slow disillusionment of their marriage.
Could she forget the first time he wasn't there for
her, or she for him? Or those dark nights later, when
they'd gone ahead and made love without enough
feeling, enough sharing? Could she forget—just
long enough to enjoy the physical love she and
Ryan used to have?

The fingers tightening through hers made her
breath come in shallow spurts. The touch was so
electric that she even thought there might still be a
chance for them. Almost against her will, her fingers closed on his stronger ones, and with the pads
of her fingertips she felt smooth skin that was hot
with loving warmth.

His voice was so hoarse it cracked. "C'mon."

"Where?"

His words were low, as throaty as they were seductive. "You know where."

No one in the thinning crowd noticed their move toward the staircase, no more than they'd remarked the kiss. When she and Ryan reached the upstairs hallway, Joy stopped. She'd seen this same look of intent in Ryan's deep brown eyes enough times to know that his mind was already made up. They were going to bed.

She bit her lower lip to stop its trembling. The trouble was, she thought dizzily, that she wanted Ryan to do every single one of those things she was imagining.

It was why she'd married him.

She hazarded a panicked glance over her shoulder, into dark eyes that made her heart race. Yes, the man definitely had lovemaking on the brain. Ryan Holt always got his way, too.

And that was the main reason she'd divorced him.

Turning, she stared blindly at an old sepia-toned photograph of the inn that decorated the hallway, thinking she had to do the logical thing—the *necessary* thing, she told herself—and go back downstairs. And then her mind went temporarily blank since Ryan wrapped his arms around her from behind, clasping his hands at her waist. "Remember how you used to garden?" he whispered against her neck.

How could the man talk about gardening at a time like this? She had no idea why he'd done so until she noticed the photograph. In it, water fell over a three-tiered white fountain that was surrounded by circular stone walkways laid with flower beds. Looking at some tea roses, she managed a nod. She did used to love gardening. In fact, she'd first gone to Stern, Wylie and Morrow to edit gardening books. Only when that division folded, had she wound up working on children's books. In the past, she'd organized tenants to plant on the roof of her and Ryan's building, too. And in the early days, they'd relax outside after work, watching Christy on the jungle gym. When had life gotten so complicated that Joy had quit growing flowers?

"I miss it," she admitted.

"I miss a lot of things."

The raw quality of Ryan's voice sent another spurt of urgency through her, as did the soft, moist kiss he planted in the hollow beneath her ear. Powerless, she found herself turning in his arms. Briefly hugging her, Ryan then caught her hands once more, backing down the hallway and pulling her, his serious-looking eyes fixed on hers, his voice almost rough. "Your room or mine, Joy?"

Her heart was hammering so hard that her throat ached. "Where's yours?"

He jerked his head. "There."

His was closer. "Yours."

She drew in a nervous breath as he swung open the door, drew her through, then kicked it shut. The room was warm and cozy, with a braided rug and a lit fire. Looking around, she started telling herself *not* to slow down, *not* to think.

It was fairly easy to do.

With the bedroom door shut, everything was a foregone conclusion. They'd known each other long enough to forget small talk and missed each other's bodies enough not to waste another breath. Ryan closed the curtain, cordoning them in the glow of the fire. Her throat closed up tight as he came toward her, matter-of-factly reaching for the waistband of her skirt as his mouth found hers. Immediately, he was moaning against her lips, pushing out his tongue and driving it down deep. One of her hands slid under his hair, raking his scalp and then pressuring his nape, begging his mouth to close even harder over hers. Her other hand went at the big gold buttons on his velvet shirt. In seconds, her palms were smoothing chest hairs, and she gasped as her own costume jacket opened and he held her breasts.

If it was cold, she didn't notice anymore. He leaned back, their hips still locked, and he felt so hot through his clothes that he seemed to burn right through her. His eyes closed halfway, smoldering, too, and her heart seemed to stop as he looked at her breasts.

''Too small,'' she'd always complained.

But he loved them. They were high and firm, with rosy pink tips. ''Peppermint candy,'' he'd whispered once. ''Let me taste.'' Now bending close, he fastened his mouth to them as if they were tasty treats, gently sucking each tightened bud in turn, then laving them until Joy begged him to pull harder with gulping draughts that flooded her. The sensations had sent her hands sliding down his bare, hairy chest, and she grasped first his belt buckle then his fly, while he yanked down the zipper of her skirt.

"Ryan," she gasped, "I'm ready...I'm so ready." As what was left of the heavy velvet costumes hit the floor, her hand quickly molded over his snug briefs and hard sex.

"Oh...thank you." Ryan gasped at her touch, briefly lifting his lips from her breast long enough to huskily utter the words of pure relieved bliss. Arching his hips for her hand, she knew he'd feared they'd never be together like this again. Maybe he couldn't live without it any more than she could. *Are we really divorced?* She suddenly thought senselessly. *Why? Why? Why?*

Ryan's fingers wiped out her memory. They curled over her hand, pressuring where she caressed him intimately. Wantonly, she opened her legs for him, then shivered as his hand brushed the triangle of hair. He gave a begging groan that shook her, then possessed her mouth once more, stormily capturing it, wetly stroking it with his tongue. He slid down his briefs, and the hot, smooth feel of him against her belly made her press against him with abandon, as did the fingers that threaded in her curls again. The one he pushed inside with thrusting motions left her mewling throatily against his shoulder. "Oh, Ryan."

His voice hitched with need. "You missed me, didn't you?"

Missed him? She was seesawing on climax—and maybe because of that unable to stop the words closest to her heart. "Ryan, has there been anybody...anybody else?"

"No." And then as if the thought were totally repelling, "God no, Joy!" Withdrawing his intimate touch, he left her right on the brink because he needed to grab her and hold her tight, hugging her whole body to him.

"There was no one else," he vowed hoarsely, urging her toward the bed. "No one."

Firelight played over his face as he came between her legs, his eyes looking dazed. His weight was on his elbows, and heat pulsed through the trembling fingertips resting on her shoulders. Drawing a bracing breath, she felt the powerful unsheathed warmth of his erection, then the slow, sweet, merciless penetration that was spreading her, followed by a faster, deeper thrust that filled her with emotion and brought tears to her eyes. "Make love to me," she gasped. "Oh, Ryan, make love to me."

"I am," he moaned, his swelling answering thrust filling her again, instantly making her shatter. Because that's the way it was with Joy and Ryan Holt.

They belonged together.

Chapter Three

Joy's head was pounding. Bits and pieces of last night's party were jumbling in her mind—swirling red and green lights, the sweet scents of ham and turkey, how funny one particular man had looked who'd been dressed as a snowman. Slowly opening an eye, Joy was sure she was in New York, and that she'd been dreaming.

But no, this was reality. *Cold* reality, Joy amended, shivering under the heavy quilt. Despite the closed patchwork curtains, the homey room was filled with gray morning light. The fire had burned out. Slowly everything came back: getting canned by Melinda, riding down Madison Avenue, flying to North Carolina…

Sleeping with Ryan!

The insistently dangerous thud of Joy's heart further awakened her. Wow, she must have had a sex dream brought on by loosened inhibitions due to the toddies. Yes, yes, of course. That's all it was. *Now* she remembered those three hot drinks. *Now* she remembered what a horribly stressful day she'd had. After all, she wouldn't…couldn't. Not with her *husband!*

Ex-husband, corrected a little voice.

Besides, who else would you do it with? another little voice said.

Had she?

As she rolled soundlessly onto her other side, she realized she was naked under the covers, and she remembered Ryan's lovemaking, too—the ravenous power of the first time, the gentle tenderness of the second.

It *seemed* real.

She quit rolling and stared, her eyes wide, her jaw slack. *Deep breath,* she thought, slowly inhaling to calm herself as she took in the prone, barely covered, obviously naked male beside her.

It really *was* her husband.

He was snoring away. His arms were above his head, elbows bent, hands clasped behind his neck. Her eyes trailed from his chiseled face, over the smooth undersides of his toned biceps, down the T of curly dark brown hair on his olive complected chest. He always worked out, and lying around in the California sun had given his well-honed body even more than the usual sheen of health. Probably he'd been jogging on the beach. Her eyes settled on the tan line, a sexy rim of lighter skin beneath his navel. Inches further down, the sheet lay across his waist and draped over him, swaddling a sex that was full and powerful, even while he slept. If it was cold in the room, the man was definitely oblivious.

And to think I was sure I'd never see him again.
Propping herself on an elbow, Joy studied his face
even though she knew the features by heart. No, he
hadn't changed a bit, she thought, sleepily, taking
in the neatly curved brown eyebrows, short thick
eyelashes, and sharp cheekbones that dipped to
shadowy cheeks. Brown stubble peppered his jaw
up to his trimmed sideburns, and above his upper
lip was the hint of the mustache he'd grown overnight.

And the hat.

Oh, yes. Now Joy remembered. When the red
velvet Santa Claus hat with the furry white ball had
fallen off, she'd plopped it on Ryan's head again
and giggled.

Now the Santa hat was tilted at a ridiculous angle, and Ryan's straight dark hair stuck straight out
from beneath it, making him look carelessly di-
sheveled. And oh so sexy. She couldn't help imagining that she'd caught Santa sneaking down the
chimney last night and that he'd slept over.

Joy eyed the door, feeling the sudden impulse to
slip from the room and think this through. Had
Ryan really come here seeking reconciliation?
Were they really back together now?

Why doubt it, Joy?

Her heart swelled as she tilted her head this way
and that, scrutinizing him. He looked so good.
"And he's so sweet," she whispered breathlessly.
He must have really flown here last night, just because he'd wanted to spend Christmas with her.

Given the raw, hungry quality of their lovemaking, how had they waited so long to get back together? Swallowing around a lump in her throat, she watched his dark eyelashes flutter, then she felt suddenly warm as half-open slits of eyes drifted over her bare shoulders.

Ryan's lips parted, lifting slightly in a smile. "Hey, Joy-to-the-world."

The sleepy throatiness of his voice sent a shiver between her shoulder blades. "I can't believe you followed me here," she found herself whispering. Leaning, she brushed a fluttery kiss by his temple. Her voice caught with emotion. "You're so romantic, Ryan." Their lovemaking had been, too. Even in the early days, she didn't think Ryan had ever been quite so sensitive as last night, or so concerned with her pleasure.

He sniffed groggily. "Followed you?"

"Well, yes…" Her heart skipped a beat. Had she misunderstood? She thought back, trying to remember what he'd actually said. Come to think of it, he'd only said he'd missed her. "I thought you and Christy got my travel information from the concierge…" At the look on his face, her voice trailed off.

Still leaning on her elbow, she watched him blink and shimmy up, propping himself against the heavy scrolled wooden headboard. That was something else new, she thought with a sudden frown. The old Ryan Holt was up and at 'em by five a.m. The new Ryan was still in bed, looking unrushed and sleepy.

He didn't even bother to glance at the bedside clock. Or notice that he was still wearing the silly Santa hat. Somehow, it was disconcerting.

"You called Mr. Hall, right?" she clarified, feeling strangely compelled to grip the covers to her breasts. "You know, the concierge from our...I mean my building?"

Ryan merely sniffed and resituated himself again, this time pulling enough of the quilt with him so that he could sit cross-legged with the covers bunched in his lap held in a loose fist.

"I didn't call Mr. Hall. Why would you think I called Mr. Hall?"

"Well, I..." She squinted at him. "You didn't call Mr. Hall?"

He rubbed his eyes. "Nope."

Which meant he hadn't followed her here, hoping for a reconciliation. Joy's hand tightened on the covers. "Then, uh...what are you doing here?"

He glanced away and stared at the blank wall for a second, as if trying to make the question make sense, then his gaze found hers again. He draped a muscular arm along the headboard. "What do you mean, what am I doing here?"

"I mean," she repeated, fixing him with her eyes, "what are you doing here?"

"I'm here for the same reason you're here."

She was afraid to ask. "Which is?"

They stared at each other another long moment. He finally said, "You're here to get Christy, right?"

"Christy?" Now Joy shimmied up, feeling much more awake. Angling her bare back against the headboard, she kept her breasts covered. "Did you say Christy?"

"You know." His dark eyes settled on hers. "Our daughter."

"I know who she is, Ryan."

He shook his head, as if to dispel some remaining sleep-muzziness. "Joy—" Gazing down at the rumpled sheet in his lap, he shook his head. "Somehow, I don't think we're connecting this morning."

Definitely not the way we were last night. "I thought you brought Christy with you."

Ryan looked into her eyes again. "I don't know what you're talking about, Joy. Christy ran away."

Joy gasped. Realizing she'd temporarily released the covers, she snatched them again, bringing them all the way up to her throat this time. "What!"

"Didn't Sheriff Warwick get ahold of you?"

Who? Joy felt completely confused. She suddenly blinked, trying to process what Ryan was saying. "Wait a minute. Did you just say Christy *ran away?* You mean from home?"

"From where else?"

Impossible. "Is she—"

"She's fine. Nothing happened to her. Sheriff Warwick said—"

"Sheriff Warwick?" Joy was beginning to feel like an idiot, parroting every word Ryan said. Why hadn't Ryan told her last night that their daughter had run away? *Because he thought you knew, Joy! He thought you came here for Christy, too.*

Which meant Ryan definitely hadn't come here to reconcile. The realization made her feel strangely sick. Last night, they'd gone at each other with nothing more than animal need. He'd said he missed her, but now she understood he'd only meant physically. She could barely find her voice. "Who's Sheriff Warwick?"

"Steve Warwick. The sheriff of Holiday Hamlet."

She simply stared, wanting to cry. Dammit, Ryan hadn't been the least interested in starting over. He'd happened on her, and he'd wanted just exactly what he'd taken.

I took, too. A flush stole over her cheeks.

"Joy?"

Deep breath. She drew one, avoiding his eyes. It was all too much to process. "So Christy came to Holiday Hamlet?"

Ryan was squinting at her. "Uh…yeah."

She nodded. Holiday Hamlet, she thought again, still feeling devastated and trying to orient herself. After Jon Sleet's children's books hit the *New York Times* bestseller's lists, the town fathers officially renamed Jon's hometown. They'd revamped Main Street, too, so that it resembled the magical Christmas town Jon described in his stories, a move that had lured in tourists. At least until Jon's wife and child had died and he quit writing. Which was why Joy was here. Shaking her head as if to clear it of confusion, she said, "Let me just get this straight. Christy—our *daughter*—ran away?"

Ryan stared at her. "Joy, she's been gone for days."

"Days? What? I mean, she—"

"Her plane was grounded near here due to a snowstorm. Instead of staying in the airport, she took a cab to Jon Sleet's house." Ryan paused and shrugged. "As near as I can figure, Christy wanted to meet him because she loves his books...."

Joy listened numbly while Ryan reiterated his conversation with the sheriff. Fear shot through her as the truth registered, then guilt because she felt like such a terrible mother. While it was true that Christy loved Jon's books, Joy couldn't believe their little girl would actually run away.

It seemed as inconceivable as last night's farce. How had she fooled herself into thinking Ryan had come here to patch up their romantic life?

By the time he quit talking, Joy was battling despair. She'd failed Elayne and Christy. Ryan and their marriage. She knew now that she was still in love with him, but while he missed her, he didn't want her back. As tears welled in her eyes, she realized she was staring wistfully at the bare chest she was never going to touch again. Suddenly her heart missed a beat. "She's at Jon Sleet's right now?"

Ryan nodded. "Yeah."

Joy's gaze shot toward the rumpled costumes on the floor. "We've got to get dressed right now and get out of here. Sometimes SWM sends people to ask Jon to write again, but ever since his wife died, he's been holed up like a hermit, angry at the whole world.'' Her voice suddenly caught. ''Around the office, the rumor is that he's in pretty bad shape, a complete recluse. His house isn't a good place for Christy.''

''Christy's fine,'' Ryan countered. ''The sheriff vouched for Jon. He's gotten his life back together. He's engaged and his fiancée's there, too. She's taken a real shine to Christy— Hold it.'' Ryan eyes widened with wakefulness, gaining their usual intelligent sharp focus and making him look more like the old Ryan Holt—the man who easily decimated miles of land with a charming grin and a quick handshake. ''If you didn't come for Christy,'' he said, ''then what *did* you come here for?''

She thought they should get moving, but Ryan's eyes demanded a response. ''I came to see about getting Jon Sleet to write for SWM again,'' she admitted.

Ryan leveled her with a long, hard stare. ''You're *working!*''

This was definitely the old Ryan—the one who was hot-tempered, jumped to conclusions and made judgments before all the facts were in. ''Well,'' she shot back temperamentally, telling herself it was high time she stood up to Ryan Holt, ''why not work? If you'll recall, I was alone on Christmas because my husband left me—''

''Don't lay that at my feet. You railroaded me

out of the apartment, Joy. You *wanted* me to leave.''

Angrily, she snatched the covers closer to her chest. "I wanted no such thing!"

His voice rose. ''That's the problem, isn't it? You want everyone else to take responsibility for your needs, your wants, your desires, your—'' He suddenly stopped.

Now, that was very *un*-Ryan-like. Usually he kept going until he worked himself into a murderous fury.

''Deep breath,'' he said.

Tilting her chin down, Joy peered at him. For years, she'd had the bad habit of verbalizing involuntary gestures when she felt tense. Aloud, she'd often find herself saying, *deep breath, deep sigh,* or *long pause.* Their daughter had picked up the habit, but Ryan never had. Until now. Staring curiously at him, Joy wondered if he'd suddenly fallen ill. When he shut his eyes and clasped his hands in his lap, and his broad shoulders and bare chest rose and fell with his deep, even breathing, she felt strangely unsettled. Somehow, this new Ryan worried her. Had the Ryan she'd known and loved really changed so much in the past eight months?

''Are you okay?'' she ventured in a whisper. ''Uh...Ryan?''

When he opened his eyes, his voice was calm. ''Yes?''

''Are you all right?''

His already dark eyes turned an angry shade

darker, but his tone was controlled. "No, not really. I can't believe you ran off to North Carolina without telling anyone but Mr. Hall."

"We're not married, Ryan," she warned softly. "And even if we were, I don't have to give you a full accounting of my every waking moment."

"Every waking moment? Our daughter's been gone for a *week!*"

Joy's heart pounded as her mind flew back to the issue at hand. "A *week?* Christy's plane was grounded a *week* ago?"

Ryan had the nerve to look vindicated. "I wish you'd called to see if she'd landed safely at L.A.X."

Joy had wanted to avoid talking to Ryan. Even now—especially now, after last night—nothing more than his deep, rumbling voice was tearing at her heart. "*You* didn't exactly call me when she didn't land."

"No, because Christy phoned and said the plans had changed."

"And you believed her?"

"Of course."

"Oh, Ryan," Joy snapped back in censure. Since the divorce, Christy had become impossible to discipline. Even Ryan could admit that the apple of their eye wouldn't tell the truth if her life depended on it.

Joy figured that Ryan probably dreaded talking to her, too. That's why he hadn't asked to speak with her on the phone.

"I thought you knew she was gone," he suddenly said. "And I...I can't believe you came here to talk to Jon about his career, especially during the holidays."

She shot him a long, sideways glance. "C'mon. Remember the old saying about stones and glass houses? I mean, let's not start talking about which one of us puts business before Christmas."

The fist in his lap closed more tightly over the quilt. "I did and I'm sorry about it."

The admission was something, but Joy knew better than to back down. If she did, she'd be in Ryan's arms again. Dangerous, when obviously nothing between them had really changed. "You're *sorry?*" She sighed. "Well, I guess that solves everything." Not that she'd ever let him off the hook for walking out of their marriage to pursue his career. "You don't even know how seriously Christy's been affected by your leaving," she added, righteously thinking he wasn't the only one who could place blame. "She'll try any ploy to get attention. For months, she fell asleep crying, while I tried to convince her that her daddy still loved her."

Ryan's voice caught with emotion. "Be fair, Joy. Christy and I are closer now than we've ever been."

After he moved, Ryan *had* started taking a real interest. He'd call and talk to Christy on the phone for hours. "I admit I didn't know she was here," Joy said. "But I did come here because of her, indirectly. I got fired, and if I don't get my job back, I'll never be able to support two girls.''

"Melinda fired you?"

Ryan's incredulous look made Joy suddenly sorry she'd introduced her professional problems. Wasn't it humiliating enough that she'd misunderstood Ryan's intentions last night? Telling him she'd failed at her job, too, only added insult to injury. Her throat suddenly closed with emotion. How could she have been so wrong? She'd pictured Ryan mooning over her in L.A., feeling lonely and depressed, arranging Christy's gifts under the tree and remembering their Christmases together. Suddenly, she'd imagined, he'd decided to hop on a plane and come for her.

It *is* Christmas, she thought with a start. Between the shock at awakening next to Ryan and worry over Christy, it had barely registered. Suddenly she didn't care that last night had reopened old wounds, intensifying the pain she felt over the separation. Her voice softened. "Merry Christmas, Ryan."

He sighed with what sounded like wistfulness. "Merry Christmas, Joy."

For a second, they were silent again, gazing at each other over the scant foot of rumpled covers. She became aware of the chill in the room, maybe because his eyes were so warm on her bare shoulders. Nothing more than the gaze, which now drifted to where the covers were against her breasts, brought heat into her skin, a soft rose flush.

Suddenly she wished she wasn't so conscious of

their nakedness. Not to mention their shared emotions. No matter what their problems, they were responsible people and would always remain united in their love for Christy.

"We'd better go get her," Joy finally said, eyeing the velvet costume that Ryan had stripped from her last night, which now lay in a crumpled heap on the floor. How was she going to get dressed? She may have slept with Ryan for years, but they were divorced now. Under the circumstances, she wasn't moving first, not without the covers. She could *take* the covers, but that would leave Ryan exposed.

Lacking her modesty, Ryan moved first, and Joy's breath caught at the sudden view of his nicely rounded shoulders, narrow waist and firm behind. He had light olive skin, the kind that looked soft, supple and glowed. When he turned around, she quickly averted her eyes and scrambled from bed— but not before she glimpsed the naked front of him. Even though she'd seen him naked countless times, her heart seemed to stop. He was so powerfully built, his sex full even when he wasn't aroused. He was aroused now, however. Her heart hammered dangerously hard against her ribs. Maybe he hadn't been as impervious to their nakedness as she'd thought.

Deep breath.

Firmly she assured herself that this was simply Ryan's usual state when he got up in the morning. It had far more to do with his dreams than her, just as last night had far more to do with his basic needs. Often, especially in the first years of their marriage, he'd slowly, sensuously awaken her by making love, and now she drew a shuddering breath, recalling how profusely he'd apologize, too, saying he should have let her sleep. As if she'd minded!

Looking completely unaware of the state of his body, Ryan turned away again, pulling back the curtains and letting some weak morning light in. "Snow's stopped."

"Good," she said as casually as she could, snatching clothes from the floor. Hardly wanting to linger, she ignored the underwear and hastily pulled on the velvet skirt and jacket. She grabbed her shoes. "What time is it?"

"Eight."

Still early. The practical turn of conversation made her heart ache. So many mornings, they'd talked just like this. Last night, she'd thought they were back together, that future mornings would be full of such easy, domestic conversation. Glancing up, she saw that Ryan had thankfully wrapped a towel from the bathroom around his waist. "I've got a rental car," he said. "We can take it to Jon's."

"Why don't we take mine?" she suggested, heading for the door, thinking she was sick of being a passenger when it came to her relationship with Ryan Holt. Literally and figuratively Ryan always did the driving. Before he could respond, she forged on. "I'll meet you downstairs in a half hour."

"An hour," he countered.

"We have to get Christy!"

"True. But you've never gotten ready in a half hour. I'm just being realistic."

"A half hour," she repeated.

He sighed. "Fine."

"See you then," she returned. Only after she'd said it did Joy realize she'd used her business voice—as if they had a meeting. When the door was shut behind her, she took off at a run. She'd make it downstairs in a half hour if it killed her.

When she was halfway down the hallway, she heard his voice behind her. "Joy?"

She turned to where he was framed in the doorway, still naked except for the towel. He said, "About last night..."

She fought the humiliated color rising in her cheeks. Had she really thought he'd come all the way out here, just to get her back? Oh, sure they'd missed each other. How could they not after eight years of marriage? They were good together, and they'd probably always love each other. But they weren't in love anymore. "Really—" She raised a staying hand. "I think we have enough trouble right now, without rehashing that."

He surveyed her for a long moment.

And then she headed for her room.

FORTY-FIVE MINUTES, Joy thought. She glanced down at her watch—last year's Christmas gift from Ryan—then across the front desk. She would have made it downstairs sooner, but there'd been no soap or shampoo in her bathroom, so she'd had to come downstairs for some. Then, as she'd showered, Joy had caught herself simply standing there, thinking about Christy. How could she make her little girl happier? And how would Christy and Elayne hit it off?

"My husband's already gone?"

Pam Scudder smiled. Between her granny glasses and wiry silver hair that was pulled into a loose bun, Pam looked more like Mrs. Claus than Joy ever could have. As Pam smoothed the front of a brand-new red housedress that was probably a Christmas gift from Hub, unwanted emotion twisted inside Joy. For the first Christmas in years, she realized, she and Ryan wouldn't be exchanging gifts.

"Honey child," Pam was saying, ignoring Joy's question, "I meant to tell you when you came down for the soap, me 'n Hub sure owe you poor kids an apology for checking you in separatelike." Leaning, she patted Joy's arm and chuckled. "'Course you two found each other last night. Still, don't you worry. As soon as your husband went to warm up the car for you, and as soon as you came down, I sent Hub to move your suitcases into the same room."

Fighting down panic, Joy said, "Please...I appreciate your help, Mrs. Scudder, but—"

"No buts, 'cause it's no trouble a'tall."

Joy merely nodded. The Scudders were so sweet. Besides, who knew what would happen by tonight?

Probably Joy and Ryan would be on separate planes and headed home, one of them with Christy.

We'll be going to different homes.

The acknowledgment hurt more than it should have. Why couldn't she simply let go of her love for Ryan? For family life? Why had she risked making love last night, since it only opened old wounds and longings? Forcing her mind to stay in the present, Joy said, "He went out to warm up the car for me?"

"Sure did. Said you get cold easy."

That admission made her heart pull, too. Ryan's warming the car was the kind of thing he used to do, the kind of thing that went by the wayside somewhere along the way. Where, Joy wasn't sure. One day, she and Ryan had simply awakened to find that they no longer did things for each other anymore…at least not the little things that mattered.

Inhaling deeply, Joy glanced around. Through an archway, she could see no signs of the party. Everything was gone—drink glasses and food, lace tablecloths and the buffet tables. From this angle, not even the Christmas tree was visible. Somehow, staring into the clean room made her feel empty inside, the way she felt when she went to the closet and found Ryan's clothes gone. The absence of his things—the shaving brush he never used, the sports equipment she was always telling him to put away—jarred her sometimes. She'd suddenly pause in a room, vaguely wondering if their marriage had really happened at all. Of course, Christy was always there, a reminder.

"You okay, honey child?" said Pam.

Joy blinked, glancing up. "Fine."

"Your husband said you two didn't have time for breakfast, 'cause ya'll gotta hit the road. Sheriff Warwick got it plowed this morning, by the way, in case you was worried. Anyhow, I fixed you 'n Ryan a bag of hot sausage biscuits and coffee. That oughtta put at least a little something in your stomachs for the drive up to Jon's."

Just the simple kindness touched Joy, and for the second time in twenty-four hours, she wondered if she'd spent too many years in New York. She loved the city, and yet the people could be so rushed and hostile. Quickly she pushed aside the thought. After all, New York was home now. And yet things here seemed so much more relaxed; people seemed kinder, less on guard. "Thanks for breakfast, Mrs. Scudder, but you didn't have to—"

"'Course I did. Least I could do for your husband."

Joy couldn't help but smile. Over the years, she'd watched a lot of women take a shine to Ryan Holt. He had good looks, a potentially soft heart, and while his commanding air sometimes drove Joy crazy, he knew how to open doors, wine and dine, and generally protect females.

Pam continued, "I mean what, with him buying the inn and all this morning…"

Joy didn't bother to hide her surprise. "Ryan bought the inn?"

"Made plans to, anyway. He didn't tell you?"

Joy shook her head.

Pam leaned her elbows on the front desk. "That feller of yours is a man on the git-go, all right. Hub heard from the sheriff that he was big into real estate out in L.A. So then Hub got to thinkin' Ryan might want to buy the inn, since me 'n Hub are dead set on retirement. Figured if your husband knows so much, he could get some folks interested in runnin' the place. You know, honey child, the kind of down-home folks that'll take good care of it. We sure will miss this old inn."

Joy kept her voice calm. "And my husband said he'd find such people for you?"

"Sure did. Came in about six a.m. Had himself a glass of milk in the kitchen with me 'n Hub."

"Six?"

Pam Scudder nodded. "Said he's an early riser, that you're the sleeper."

Six. When Joy awakened, she should have known Ryan was only taking a nap. He must have gone out for a jog, then returned, undressed and plopped the Santa hat on his head again. It wasn't yet nine and her husband—ex-husband, she reminded herself—had already bought an inn, was on his second breakfast and was outside, warming up the car for her. "Did he go running?" Joy couldn't help but ask.

Pam nodded. "Sure did, honey child. That's when me and Hub saw him. Running in this weather!'' Pam exclaimed, sounding scandalized. "And in those skimpy little shorts!''

"That'd be Ryan," Joy said dryly.

The same Ryan, she thought, who was going to take these nice people for a ride. Maybe he hadn't changed at all. What if he'd gotten even more cut-throat in his new realty job?

Joy fought the queasiness in her stomach. Not to mention her torn loyalties. She and Ryan were divorced, but she hardly felt comfortable intervening in his business dealings. Still, Pam and Hub Scudder were the salt of the earth. "Uh...Mrs. Scudder," Joy finally said diplomatically. "Before you sign any papers with my husband, you might want to check into some of his past deals."

"Past deals?"

"Well, he has worked mostly with larger projects. You know, big city developments."

Mrs. Scudder obviously loved the old inn. She ran a worried hand through her silver hair. "He said he bought land out in the country, though, honey child. Said his old office had done bought up farm country in Georgia, and some seafood restaurants in Florida."

"Well...his old realty company did." And they'd built high-rise condos, strips malls and fast-food franchises. Joy managed a shrug. "It's just good business practice to check it out. You know, before you make big life decisions."

Pam smiled. "You'd be right about that, but there's not much we can do on Christmas day."

Christmas. Joy glanced through a window at the gray morning, thinking that Christy was supposed to have awakened her and Ryan today. By now, they'd be drinking coffee, watching their excited daughter tearing the paper off her gifts. Instead Christy had run away.

"Here." Cutting off her thoughts, Joy scribbled a number. "You can call here on Christmas." It was the home number of Ryan's ex-boss in New York.

"He'd give your husband references on Christmas?"

Ryan's ex-boss had absolutely no life outside the office, and he'd be more than happy to brag about his and Ryan's land conquests and acquisitions. "The man would talk to you at *four a.m.* on Christmas, Mrs. Scudder."

"Well, thanks to ya."

"No problem."

At least it wasn't until Joy turned around to find Ryan staring at her, his eyes murderous. He wasn't but five feet away, freshly-scrubbed and clean-shaven, his cheeks ruddy from the cold. With his jeans, he was wearing a V-neck sweater she'd gotten him last year for his birthday, and a waist-length, fleece-lined jacket and hiking boots, neither of which she'd seen before. Stepping forward, he wordlessly slid his hand beneath her elbow and gave Mrs. Scudder a wincing smile. As he man-handled Joy toward the door, he said under his breath, "I can see you've got a real high opinion of me."

She kept her voice low. "You're about to turn a very nice couple out of an inn they love!" She drew away, but Ryan held her elbow tight. Maybe it was just as well, since when they got outside, her boots were slick on the ice.

"So, you're driving after all, as usual," she said as he veered away from her car in the parking lot.

"I didn't have your keys," he returned. "And I wanted to warm up the car for you. And, Joy," he added, "you have no idea why I bought that inn."

"Enlighten me." Her eyes shot to his, and her heart did that awful, sickening flip-flop again. *Please,* she thought with sudden desperation. *Tell me it's not true.* "What were your plans for the property?"

He shrugged as he opened the passenger side of his rental car, a beat-up heap he'd usually never be caught dead in. Strange, Joy thought, once she was inside and he'd slammed the door, driving such a car didn't seem to bother him in the least.

"Well," she said when Ryan got in his side and slammed the door, "are you going to tell me what you're going to do with the inn?"

"No," he said simply.

"So much for the new Ryan Holt," she murmured.

"What's that supposed to mean."

She shrugged, staring through the windshield

he'd already scraped. "For a minute there, I thought you'd changed."

He turned the key in the ignition, making the engine of the old car rattle to life. "Maybe I have."

Maybe. But Ryan hadn't come here because he'd realized he was still in love with her. And really, maybe she didn't want him back, either. No, she assured herself, of course she didn't. Besides, she and Ryan had other concerns.

As soon as Ryan negotiated the mountains looming before them, she'd get her daughter and go home.

Chapter Four

"Excited hop!" Clutching the binoculars so they wouldn't bang against her chest, Christy jumped into the air, whirled around breathlessly, then peered through a narrow upstairs window that was offset by stained-glass panels. A tan jalopy was approaching from the bottom of Mistletoe Mountain, the same car she was sure her dad had been driving last night.

"Christy?"

She glanced over her shoulder at the doorway, toward Jon's fiancée's raised voice. "Are you yelling for *moi,* Nikki?"

"Sure am. Don't you want to come down and open your presents, hon?"

Presents! Santa shouldn't have, not after last night when Christy had sat on his lap and assured him she didn't want anything except for her parents to get remarried. But Santa had put presents under the tree, anyway. How could Christy have doubted he was real? She'd turned eight years old this morning, which seemed awfully old to still believe in

Santa Claus. But hey, if the guy brought her presents and got her mom and dad back together...

A male voice shouted, "Christy?"

"Coming, Jon!" Christy yelled, keeping the binoculars trained on the tan car. Since she wasn't even supposed to know Sheriff Warwick had found her parents, she couldn't say she was waiting for her mom and dad. Not that the sheriff had been all that important to the search. He was only Santa's instrument. *Santa* was sending her parents here as a Christmas gift.

"Deep sigh." She could almost see them when they got here—kneeling on the floor, holding her hands and speaking in quiet tones as they broke the news of their engagement.

"We know change can be difficult," her mother might say.

"But we're together again, and that's what matters," her dad would add.

Christy was going to have to look surprised. Lifting her eyes from the binoculars, she practiced in a nearby mirror, bugging her eyes out and stretching her mouth into an O. *"Perfecto,"* she pronounced.

She just hoped her parents weren't too mad about her running away. Of course, if they weren't home they couldn't ground her or send her to her room. But what if Nikki hadn't made enough food to invite them for Christmas dinner? Nikki had gone all out, making turkey and dressing, cranberry sauce and gravy, and homemade bread and pies. For a tomboy, she sure could cook. She'd even made Christy a birthday cake.

"Hon?" Nikki yelled. "Are you playing with that godawful boa constrictor again?"

"Uh...yeah." Noodles was really in the other room, twining around the stick Jon had put in the aquarium. "Wince," Christy whispered guiltily. Her parents were going to be upset when they realized that her friend Kelly wasn't really baby-sitting Noodles, and that Christy had smuggled him through airport security.

"Hon, we're going to eat this afternoon," Nikki shouted. "After my dad and brothers get here from Kentucky. That okay with you?"

"Great!" Christy's frown vanished. She couldn't wait to see how Jon handled Nikki's brothers. A week ago, when Christy hopped inside Nikki's pink taxicab in front of the airport, who would have guessed that Nikki and Jon would wind up falling in love—and so fast! Of course, Nikki was pregnant with her old boyfriend's baby, but Jon said he didn't care. And now Jon was just hoping Nikki's brothers didn't show up for Christmas dinner with shotguns. Not that a shotgun wedding would be required, since Nikki had wanted a husband for Christmas, and now Jon was going to give her one—him.

Santa sure worked fast.

Which was why the tan jalopy was coming up the hill. And it was definitely her mom and dad!

Now Christy could see her father's dark hair and a blond woman beside him.

"Christy?" Jon yelled. "Did you get lost up there? Are you sure you're not getting into more mischief?"

"*Moi?* Mischief?"

"Yes, you, kiddo."

"Uh…I'm trying to figure out what to wear." She glanced down at the purple sweat suit that had once belonged to Jon's daughter. Maybe she *should* change.

Trouble was, she'd brought mostly sundresses, since she was supposed to be visiting her dad in L.A. But she did have the cute elf costume from last night, and the outfit she'd worn on the plane from New York—a red velvet dress, white leggings and gloves, with black patent leather shoes. Also, there was a calf-length green wool coat her daddy hadn't even seen yet, with velvet trim and a matching hat. Nikki said the outfit made her look like a pint-size United States first lady, and Christy didn't think it was a compliment. But then, there was no accounting for personal taste.

"Just come down," Nikki yelled. "I'm sure you look fine, hon."

Nikki *would* think so. She wore big sweaters, jeans with holes in the knees and baseball caps. For her, a sweat suit was probably swanky party wear. Christy had helped her pick out the velvet dress she'd worn last night, spritzed her with Chanel perfume Christy had stolen from her mom and shown

Nikki how to apply makeup. Without Christy's help, Nikki's romance with Jon would never have happened.

"Deep sigh of relief." Christy let her shoulders droop and blew out a long one. Shoot, she'd nearly run her short legs ragged last week, trying to get those two together.

"If you can't decide, just wear your jeans," Nikki persisted. "You might want to go outside later."

Nikki had a point. Christy might want to go sledding or show her parents the animals in the barn. Still, ever since the big D—meaning the divorce— Christy had been trying to dress better, thinking that if she cleaned up her act and looked more like a good little girl, her daddy might come home.

"But he *is* home now," she whispered, looking at the car. Or at least in love with Christy's mom again. Which meant Christy could wear the sweat suit since she didn't have to worry anymore.

Or did she?

"Gasp!" Christy exclaimed as the car pulled to the side of the road. After a panicked moment, she told herself that her parents were stopping to discuss how to break the news of their upcoming remarriage.

Christy hoped it was true.

"AND THEN THERE'S the strange way Christy's been dressing," Joy was saying as she pulled down her visor to further block the sun that had burst through the clouds. Joy usually let Ryan control things, so he was surprised when she suddenly gripped the dashboard and looked over her shoulder. "Wait a minute. Why are you pulling over, Ryan?"

"So we can talk better."

"You can't talk and drive?"

Not with you next to me. Her scent alone was fueling unwanted ideas about making love again, right here in the car. But Ryan knew better. How he'd found her intervening in his business dealings this morning proved the basic trust between them was gone. Besides, they weren't even talking about the issues, just treading close and backing off, sometimes conversing so politely that they could have been at one of those rooftop garden parties Joy used to host for their business associates. If a stranger was listening, he wouldn't believe Joy and Ryan had gotten naked together last night.

Ryan managed a shrug. "I'd just like to give you my undivided attention. And sorry about the car," he added. The battered compact's engine rattled as he edged onto a narrow icy shoulder between the cleared road and the high snowdrifts left by the plow. "It was the last car on the lot."

Joy's mouth stretched into a tentative, almost apologetic smile. He decided it was meant to communicate two things: that making love last night had been a grave error, and that, however unfortunately, they had to pull together and create a unified parental front now, for Christy's sake. Joy said,

"I'm sorry about the car. I confess, I'm the one who rented the second-to-last one."

He couldn't help but smile. "That'd be the one with the quiet engine and the working radio?"

"Only if you like country-western, jazzed up with static."

She knew he hated country-western. "Good thing you left this luxury ride for me."

After adjusting the heater, Ryan gripped a stiff hand crank and cracked the window. When he turned to Joy, any remaining anger he felt over her intervention with the Scudders vanished. She was definitely the same traffic-stopping Joy he'd married. Flawlessly turned out in simple basics, she was peering at him through sunglasses. He glanced over her face, at the lenses that were so dark he couldn't see her green eyes, then at her bright red lipsticked mouth. The shawl collar of the black wool coat she was bundled in hid a neck he knew was long, slender and as tasty as taffy.

"Maybe we should have brought your car," he found himself saying. "But like I said, I didn't have the keys, and I wanted to go ahead and warm it up."

At that, she looked vaguely uncomfortable, swallowed hard and glanced away—maybe remembering how fast she'd left his room this morning. Ryan took the opportunity to let his eyes drift over her hair. Last night, he'd been too rushed to notice it. Besides, it was mussed. Now he saw it was no longer parted in the middle, but on the side. It was still short, though, cut over her ears in the way he liked. But how long had it been since he'd noticed that her skin was this pale? It was like seashells that had been washed smooth, as soft and white as the snow beyond the windshield.

"Thanks," she said. "For warming up the car, I mean."

"Wouldn't want you to shiver."

She was still staring through the passenger window, at a snowy wooded mountainside, and he wondered—maybe even wished—she was remembering the shivers he'd elicited last night. "Anyway," she suddenly continued, "it was bad enough when Christy brought Noodles to the annual mother-daughter luncheon at work—"

"Christy did *what?*" On the drive, Ryan had already heard enough blood-curdling tales about their daughter's recent behavior to know he and Joy needed to start talking again. If they didn't, their wily little girl was going to keep playing both sides against the middle.

Joy glanced fleetingly at him, then through the windshield where snow flurries were falling—some collecting on the glass, some melting in the sunlight. "She brought Noodles to the luncheon in a backpack she's been carrying, and…well, I guess he got loose. So, anyway, there we were, sitting at the head table next to Melinda, and when Melinda got up to deliver her Christmas speech—"

"You mean *your* Christmas speech," Ryan interjected. Then, realizing he shouldn't have said it, he added, "Too warm?"

"No, not really."

But she was. He watched as Joy unbuttoned and shimmied out of her coat, and he leaned, to help slip it from her shoulders. Beneath, she wore a simple black pantsuit with a white blouse and a silk scarf that was tied in a fancy knot around her neck.

He knew better, but couldn't stop himself from persisting. "C'mon, you *did* write Melinda's speech, right?"

She shot him a defensive look. "Of course I did," she returned levelly, "Melinda's my *boss*."

The boss who fired you, Ryan seethed silently. As far as he was concerned, Joy had always been too accommodating at SWM. She was always looking out for the other person, instead of for herself. She'd been the same way in their marriage. He just wished it hadn't taken him years to realize that there really was such a thing as *too* nice. "Sorry," he said now. "I didn't mean to interrupt."

Slight color stained her cheeks—an admission that she knew the issue was deeper than Melinda. "You can't bring up something like that and just drop it, Ryan. You *always* said I did too much for Melinda, but—"

"You *did* do too much for her." *And for me.* "In order to get the raises and promotions Melinda promised, didn't you always have to go over her head, to Stern or Wylie?"

"Maybe." She crossed her arms. "But not anymore, seeing as I don't even have a job."

Even though he knew better than to judge or offer unwanted opinions, Ryan was getting steamed. "I can't believe you actually want that job back."

"It's a good job."

"Manhattan's a big town. There're lots of good jobs. That's why we decided to live there."

"Ryan, not everybody eats nails for breakfast. I'm just not as assertive as you, okay?"

"Sorry." And he was. "So Noodles got out," he said, putting the conversation back on track.

"Yeah."

"And?"

Suddenly Joy's shoulders shook with suppressed laughter. As fine as it was to see her good humor return, even that unnerved him. Just once, why couldn't Joy really light into him? Tell him to keep his opinions to himself? Tell him her professional life was none of his damn business? Really, it wasn't anymore, since they were divorced.

"Well...Melinda screamed." Glancing at him, Joy took off her sunglasses, and the sparkle in her clear green eyes made his heart stutter. "I mean, at the top of her lungs. By then, she was only inches from the microphone, too."

He stared at Joy. "Melinda screamed into the microphone instead of starting the speech?"

"Deafening," Joy assured with another chuckle. "Everybody in the company swore they couldn't hear for the next week. Even the people in contracts heard her, and you know they're all on the forty-ninth floor. One guy even said he'd made an appointment to be fitted with hearing aids.''

Ryan's lips tugged into a smile. ''I know you like Melinda, sweetheart, but I say it serves her right.''

Joy giggled in a mischievous way that reminded him of their daughter. ''Well, then, you'll love what happened next.''

His eyes widened. ''That wasn't the end of it?''

''Oh, no. If it was, I might still have a job. After Melinda screamed—'' Joy paused, both for effect and to release a soft peal of laughter that reminded him of a million reasons why he loved her. ''She passed out. I swear to you, Ryan, she dropped to the floor in a dead faint. Even *that* would have been okay, but...''

During another jingling peal of merriment that kept her from continuing, Ryan realized how much he missed her ability to milk a story. ''But what? Tell me.''

When Joy could control herself, she said, ''Well, this new v.p. of finance, one of those gray-suited corporate types, comes running over and starts giving Melinda CPR.''

''CPR?''

''Well, you can imagine! There's Melinda, with her perfect hair, Donna Karan suit and three-inch heels. And suddenly, this man in a gray suit is spreading her legs, so he can shove her head between them.''

A deep rumble of laughter came from Ryan's chest. "You're kidding, right?"

"I wish." Joy blushed, the way she often did whenever talking about embarrassing moments. "At least half of Manhattan—and definitely the rank-and-file at SWM—realized she was wearing underwear printed with flames."

"Flames?"

Joy nodded. "Yeah, like tongues of fire."

Ryan's shoulders shook, and then suddenly, they were laughing together. Watching her, listening to the tinkling rise and fall of her laughter, Ryan felt another thoroughly inappropriate tug of arousal. Great. He'd already been embarrassed once today. When he'd had to get out of bed, he'd been hard as a rock. How could he help it? They'd been sitting there forever talking, naked beneath the sheets.

That was the good thing about being a woman, he guessed. You could hide your responses. And this morning was so much like the old days. He'd awakened first. Seeing her naked, he'd wanted her so much that he'd slipped from bed and gone running to wear himself out. If he hadn't instituted morning workouts in the early days of their marriage, Joy never would have slept past five a.m. The second Ryan opened his eyes—always promptly at five—it took everything he had not to slide between her legs and make love to her.

Which is what he'd usually done *after* his run. At least that way, she got to sleep an extra hour.

"Anyway," Joy said when she could quit laughing, "me getting fired was hardly Christy's fault. SWM's just reorganizing again. And anyway, if I can get Jon to start writing again, then I'll probably get my old job back."

"You know how I feel," he couldn't help but say. "I wish you'd find other employment."

Sudden anger sparked in her eyes. "Why?"

The words were out before he thought them through. "Just once, I'd like to see you lose your temper. To get mad and forget Melinda's point of view. Or those of the car pool mothers who were always having last-minute crises and leaving you to escort their girls to ballet or tap or whatever."

Color crept into her cheeks. "Why does it mean so much to you, Ryan?"

Because you never voice your needs. If you did, maybe we'd have a chance. That's why I hate watching you let Melinda walk all over you. When he spoke, his voice was deceptively soft. "You know why."

"Okay," she admitted, without much energy. "I'll stand up for myself. Living with you was no picnic. Happy now?"

"No, just sorry." Hell, of the two of them, he'd been far worse. Selfish to the core. A taker. But his mother was right. Deep down, he was holding out some kind of impossible hope that things between him and Joy could change. *But they won't, Ryan. Don't fool yourself.*

Joy, who'd been staring at the quickening snow through the windshield, slid her sunglasses back on, more to hide her eyes he thought than to shield them from the sun. "Do you still want to stop?" she said, changing the subject. "The Scudders said the couple who own the toy store'll come down if we want to pick up a few things for Christy. Apparently Jon and Nikki figured out it was her birthday, so Nikki made a cake."

For a moment, Ryan simply sat there, his fingers curling around the steering wheel. He sighed. "Christy doesn't need any more presents. We've already spoiled her rotten. There's plenty in the trunk, anyway—Beanie Babies, Giga pets, an Eight ball, board games, scrunchies, jewelry—" He caught Joy's stunned expression. "Ma said you were getting her a computer, so I got tons of smaller things."

Joy twisted her hands. "I didn't realize you'd brought gifts with you. I just wish I had something for her. I want her to know how much we love her."

His voice lowered. "You can't buy love."

"I didn't mean that."

But they were both guilty of it. When Ryan made good, he'd lavished Joy with gifts, as if a pearl necklace or diamond pin could ever make up for the hours when they were working too hard, when they hadn't been talking, sharing, loving.

He shook his head. "Don't worry, before you came outside, I added your name to the gift tags."

Joy took off her sunglasses again. The way her gaze softened with surprise made him wonder again just how self-absorbed he'd been during their marriage. "Thanks," she said. "That was sweet."

And obviously unexpected. But no parent wanted to come to their kid on Christmas morning, empty-handed. He said, "We need to put on a unified front when we see her."

Joy nodded. "Okay. We'll do whatever you think best."

Right. He knew Joy was being nice, but he hated the reminder of how overly accommodating she could be. "Why don't you tell me more about what's going on? Mostly I talk to her, so I'm not getting the skinny."

"Oh, Ryan, she's been a good little girl," Joy said in a rush, as if she'd been waiting to unburden herself. "She's interested in things. But she's throwing more temper tantrums and alienating sitters. The NYPD came up one day when she was throwing water balloons onto the street…"

He listened for a while. It was a long litany.

Joy's voice was concerned. "And I don't think it's all our divorce, Ryan."

He raised an eyebrow. "No?"

She shook her head. "No. I think she's upset because Elayne's coming to live with us. And Elayne…"

Her voice trailed off. For long moments, Joy stared at where strong sun reflected off the snow-blanketed mountainside, and Ryan didn't know how to read her expression. Hell, he'd never understood her relationship to her family. No one could have craved family life more than Joy, and yet she'd barely talked to her Aunt May and Uncle Jer.

Oh, there'd been times, especially on holidays, when Joy had been strangely distant as if she needed to separate herself at family gatherings. But even now, she spoke fondly of the parents she'd lost. They'd been close. Her aunt and uncle had obviously loved her, so much that the distant tone in Joy's voice when they called had hurt him. They begged for visits, but Joy would rarely go.

When they did visit, she'd be so happy during the trip that he'd think she was enjoying herself. She, May and Jer were surprisingly close, and Joy doted on Elayne who'd been about Christy's age last time Ryan saw her. She was a beautiful kid. Like Joy, her mother, May and Christy, Elayne was small-boned, emerald-eyed and blond. On the rare visits, Ryan had been sure Joy was having fun herself…until they got home. For weeks after the trips, Joy was listless, slower to laugh. He'd hear her crying in the bathroom, or she'd come to dinner with her eyes red-rimmed. Since she'd wanted to keep her feelings private, he'd never said anything, though now he wished he had.

Ryan figured May and Jer reminded her of how she'd lost her parents, but why couldn't Joy move beyond that? May, Jer and their daughter, Elayne, had been Joy's family, as surely as he and Christy were. They loved her.

So do I.

But it no longer mattered. There was too much of herself Joy would never share. Too much that he hadn't bothered to draw out of her, the way he should have. He still had a lot of unanswered questions about what she did with money, for instance. Sometimes, it would simply disappear, and she didn't have a thing to show for it. He'd told himself it was her business. She made her own money, didn't she? But now, he wished he knew the truth.

"Ryan?"

He realized he was staring blankly through the windshield and blew out a sigh. On the subject of Elayne, Christy hadn't offered much during their phone conversations. "Wasn't Elayne supposed to be in New York by now?"

"Yeah." Joy gazed through the window, maybe thinking of the quick illness that had taken Aunt May's life.

"Well, did you talk to Elayne when you went down there to see May?"

"Not much. She was always with friends."

"Now?"

"Not much," she repeated. "Elayne said she wanted to stay in Beckley until the end of the school term, then come for Christmas."

"But she didn't come?"

"Well…she changed her mind and decided to stay with her best friend for Christmas. The Bowers are nice people. I went to school with Sally, and her husband's the minister of our old church. They wanted her to stay."

"And you wanted to do what Elayne wanted."

Joy nodded. "She's had such a rough time."

Gently Ryan couldn't help but say, "Elayne's a kid, you know. She needs guidance. She's not old enough to make all her own decisions."

"It was only one decision," insisted Joy.

The intensity of the emotion in her eyes made his whole body still. There was something so raw there, so deep. Suddenly he wanted to grab his ex-wife and hold her in a bone-crushing embrace. She looked so...uncertain? So...guilty? Whatever it was, he told himself now, was none of his business. He and Joy were only together right now because of Christy. Last night, he'd had hopes they'd get back together, and Joy apparently thought he'd followed her here. But her intervention in his business affairs proved their basic trust was gone. Besides, if Joy really wanted a reconciliation, he'd have to see her stand up and fight for it. He had to know she could voice her needs, become an equal partner in their relationship.

Not that it would happen. Ryan's heart pulled as he thought of Elayne, a little girl he barely remembered. If he and Joy were still married, he'd have become a father to her...or at least the closest thing to it. He would have liked that. For so long, he and Joy had tried unsuccessfully to have other children which is why he hadn't worried overmuch about using a condom last night.

Joy's voice suddenly shook. "Do you think I did the wrong thing about Elayne, Ryan? Do you think

I should have forced her to come for Christmas? She probably thinks her *aunt* doesn't even care.''

Her eyes begged for an answer, so much so that Ryan barely wondered over the unusual stress she'd placed on the word "aunt." How much she valued his opinion almost hurt. "What *you* think is all that matters," he said carefully. "And Christy always said…''

He paused, finding it hard to go on, wondering if his and Joy's marriage would have been different had they had other kids. He'd never know. When it came to baby-making, he and Joy were over and done with it. Toast. Even if the doctors they'd seen assured them there was no medical cause.

"Christy always said?" Joy prompted.

"That she wanted a sister.''

Another flush stained Joy's cheeks. Maybe she, too, was thinking about the babies they'd planned but never had. "Before the divorce that was true," said Joy. "But now…'' Joy glanced into her lap, picking imaginary lint off her black pants. "Now, I think she fears another child is going to take away our already limited time together. I think that's why she's clammering for attention. Like with the clothes.''

"Clothes?''

"Christy's dressing like a poster girl for the Republican party. Everything we buy has to be navy, kelly green, or gray. She wears pillbox hats, lace tights. Not that the clothes aren't nice, but…'' Joy threw up her hands. "I can't get her interested in anything she used to like."

"Has she quit wearing makeup?" Ryan asked hopefully.

"Unfortunately not. But she's quit wearing different color nail polish on every nail."

"She did that?"

Joy nodded. "It's very in. Especially in fluorescent colors."

Ryan guessed you'd have to be female to understand. "Oh."

"She even tried to throw out her leather jacket."

Ryan frowned. "She begged me to buy her that jacket. I even caught her sleeping in it once."

Joy nodded. "Well, now she's dressing very conservatively, like she's trying to be a little adult. Or a storybook good little girl." Joy's voice suddenly caught. "I keep trying to make sure she understands we love her just the way she is."

Ryan glanced toward a distant hill. According to the directions the Scudders had given, Jon Sleet lived at the top. "Well," he said. "When we get up there, let's have a sit down and ask her how she feels about Elayne."

Joy stared at him. "What?"

"I said we should have a talk." Prior to now he'd never been much good in the touchy-feely department. Maybe he still wasn't. But Ryan had spent the past eight months on a shrink's couch, carefully analyzing his life, desperately trying to figure out where his and Joy's marriage went

wrong, and what he could have done to save it.
Maybe now, he figured, he could do touchy-feely.

"It's worth a shot," he added. Then he wondered
if he meant talking to Christy or saving the marriage.

Chapter Five

"I didn't even *tell* Santa I wanted platform sneakers!" Christy exclaimed, her chin-length blond ringlets bouncing as she shoved her feet into a neon green pair. "And they fit *perfecto!*" She lifted her eyes to the ceiling. "*¡Mucho gracias,* Santa!"

"Looks good with the purple sweat suit, kid," Jon offered, stoking the fire before returning to the oversize armchair he'd been sharing with his fiancée.

Joy shot him a smile, still barely able to believe he was remarrying—or how the match had come about. As it turned out, Nikki Ryder drove the cab that brought Christy from the airport to Jon's, and when Jon claimed Christy was a runaway, Nikki had decided to stay until the Holts were found. Nikki and Jon had fallen in love.

They looked strangely compatible. He was a big man, over six feet, with sage eyes and longish chestnut hair salted with premature silver. The much smaller-boned Nikki was blissfully dwarfed by his cradling arm. She was younger, too, with a tomboyish air, but not even faded jeans, a worn sweatshirt and baseball cap could hide her stunning dark eyes, full lips and luxuriously thick, red-touched brown hair.

Hazarding another glance beside her on the comfortably worn sofa, Joy watched Ryan's face light up as Christy dived again under the bushy decorated tree. Obviously his regular phone calls had brought him and Christy much closer. The new job in L.A. had sounded higher-profile, but it wasn't so all-consuming that Ryan wasn't getting his priorities straight. Her heart suddenly pounding, Joy wished he'd done so before their marriage was over.

For the first time in years, he'd known what their daughter wanted for Christmas—and he'd fulfilled every wish. Joy was glad, even if watching Christy open the gifts was a constant reminder of how Christmases used to be. Crossing her feet on the braided rug, she set down a mug of cider and forced herself to look away from Ryan, watching Christy for a moment, then taking in the room.

It was smaller than most, warm and homey, with an inviting fire and holiday decorations. Most of the other rooms in the huge stone house were furnished with heavy ornate pieces that had been in the Sleet family for generations. Here, a simple china nativity scene sat atop the dark wood mantel from which needlepoint stockings hung. Nutcracker soldiers, Santa Clauses and ceramic angels were artlessly scattered on end tables, and prisms shaped like snowflakes dangled against the windowpanes.

"Careful there," Ryan said as Christy ran over and stacked an unwrapped dress box next to him, leaving him no choice but to scoot so close to Joy that she could feel his body heat and smell his scent. Angel Men always drove her wild.

"The ones that are marked birthday are from your mom and me, not Santa," Ryan added.

"Barbie!" Christy squealed, ignoring her dad and flinging wrapping paper to the already littered floor. "My friend, Kelly, says we're too old for Barbie dolls, but Santa knew I wanted one!" Opening a smaller package, she added, "Oh, it's a wet suit and prom dress!"

"Barbie'll sure look dolled up in those," Ryan offered.

"Dolled up." Joy chuckled.

"You think so, Daddy?" asked Christy distractedly, missing the wordplay and not really wanting a response.

The Barbie was one of many gifts Jon and Nikki had put under the tree for Christy, so Joy glanced at Jon, mouthing, "Thanks."

Jon smiled back, the brief sadness in his eyes tweaking Joy's emotions. All week, Jon and Nikki had cared for Christy while searching for her parents, and these gifts, Joy knew, had been meant originally for a daughter Jon had lost two years ago.

Despite that loss, Jon looked happy now. Nikki Ryder had helped heal wounds that Joy simply couldn't imagine. In the instant between hearing Christy had run away and being told she was safe,

Joy had known a similar true despair. So had Ryan.
Which was why they hadn't talked to Christy immediately about the seriousness of her running
away. When they saw her, all but her safety fled
their minds. Christy had run into their waiting arms,
and Joy had squeezed tight, running fingers through
Christy's silken curls. Suddenly Joy hadn't given a
damn what her baby girl had done wrong. How
could a mother act stern when she was busy thanking God her child was safe?

With only a glance, Joy and Ryan had decided
to discipline Christy later. For now, it was Christmas and her birthday. And she wanted to see her
parents together. Ryan and Joy could give her that
much. Now, Joy noticed Jon's hand tightening
around Nikki's waist. The arm Nikki had draped
around his shoulders squeezed back. *So much love,*
Joy thought. When Nikki smiled, Joy hazarded another glance at Ryan.

"More presents, Christy?" Nikki was teasing.
"Must be hard to have a birthday on Christmas.
How are you possibly going to open all these,
hon?"

Christy planted her hands on her hips, feigning a
beleaguered sigh. "Deep sigh. It's hard work, but
somebody's gotta do it."

"We thought she'd hate it," Joy commented,
taking another sip of hot cider and glancing toward
Ryan for confirmation, which he gave. "You know,
some kids feel slighted when they have a birthday
around the holidays, but when we asked Christy if

she wanted to celebrate her birthday on another day
of the year, she said no.''

"I love Christmas!'' Christy squealed, nearly
tripping over the loose sneaker laces as she bolted
for the tree again.

"We love Christmas, too,'' Joy and Ryan said in
unison as they always did. It was sort of a family
joke, since Christy's full name was Christmas.

"Love you, too,'' Christy called excitedly, whirling around to face Jon and Nikki. "C'mon, you've
got to start opening.''

Jon shrugged. "But we like watching you.''

"You two go ahead,'' Ryan urged.

"Please,'' Joy murmured. "Open your gifts.''

As Jon and Nikki exchanged glances, Joy was
conscious once more of having no gifts for Ryan
this year. Her chest swelled, aching as she watched
their daughter reading name tags on packages. How
had time passed by so quickly for them all? Just
yesterday, she and Ryan were at the New York Uni-
versity hospital, holding their seven-pound baby,
and now Christy was merrily reading tags on
Christmas gifts. Suddenly aware that Ryan had
been watching her, Joy felt rather than saw his gaze
slide away, toward the perfect, beautiful child
they'd made.

Christy had so much from each of them—the
flaxen blond hair Joy had had as a child, her eyes.
Ryan's broader forehead, fuller lips and impish
smile of surprise. His energy. His willfulness. Joy
couldn't even look at Christy without thinking of

Ryan. Or of Elayne since she, too, was blond with emerald eyes. If Elayne had features from Doug Ritts, Joy didn't know—or care. Aunt May said he'd married some years back and owned a computer store in Beckley. Not that he'd ever acknowledged Elayne. He'd made it clear he wouldn't years ago.

"Like it, Mommy?"

"Cute!" Joy exclaimed, smiling approvingly at another dress, since Christy had quit reading tags long enough to open another gift. And yet, Joy's mind was a million miles away. What was Elayne doing now? Had she liked the presents Joy sent? Soon, Joy would excuse herself to call her "niece."

"Thanks, Christy." Jon accepted some packages. "Yes, indeed. Looks like these are for me, kid." Hoarding his gifts, he leveled Christy with a proprietary glare that made her giggle. "And I'm not sharing," Jon vowed.

"They're not much, Jon," Nikki suddenly murmured apologetically, her native Kentucky twang sounding more pronounced. "I…"

"I can't wait." Jon's sage eyes lasered into hers for a long moment, communicating love that had been obvious to Joy all morning. Whenever Nikki so much as left the room to replenish drinks, Jon would wait an obligatory moment, then leave, too— no doubt to steal kisses in the kitchen.

Now Nikki frowned as Christy skipped over, bringing her two small, gold-wrapped boxes. Nikki said, "How did you…? When did you…?"

Jon's drawl was throaty. "Merry Christmas, Mrs. Sleet."

Heightened color turned Nikki's cheeks deep rose. "I'm not Mrs. Sleet yet," she reminded huskily.

"Soon enough," Jon assured.

"Have you set a date?" Joy asked, her own pulse leaping, since the smallest box had to contain jewelry. An engagement ring? she wondered, noticing Nikki's fingers were bare.

"Yeah," Jon said with a chuckle. "Yesterday." Then sobering, he added, "Whenever Nikki wants."

Joy smiled. There was such a lightness to Jon's voice now, so much wonder in his eyes when he looked at his fiancée. Just watching them, Joy thought that the power of love could change everything, heal anything. Why couldn't that happen for her and Ryan?

Nikki ran a nail under the tape of the larger of the boxes. "A new baseball cap!" she exclaimed a moment later, laughing. It was fancy and fun, covered with embroidery and tiny mirrors. Jon whipped off the cap she'd been wearing and playfully plopped the new one on her head. "Like it, Ryder?"

"Love it, Sleet." Holding the smaller box, Nikki's hands suddenly shook, and her quickening breath could be heard over some softly playing Christmas music. Pulling away the paper, Nikki gasped when she saw the white velvet ring box, and as she gently lifted the lid, her soft brown eyes filled with tears. "Oh, Jon, when…?"

"I got the owner of the jewelry store to meet me last night. It may need some sizing, but I guessed. Here, let me…" Lifting the ring, he slid it onto her finger.

Nikki's voice was barely audible. "Guess this makes it official, Sleet."

Cupping her chin, Jon turned her toward him, so he could gaze deeply into her eyes. "Oh, Ryder," he returned. "It was official the second I laid eyes on you. You just didn't know it yet."

She glanced down, swallowing hard. "And it fits."

"Chalk that up to help from Santa. Still, we'll have the jeweler look at it to make sure."

"No," Nikki whispered. "It's perfect."

"You're perfect," Jon whispered back.

Joy's eyes stung with unshed tears as she watched them kiss. God, this reminded her so much of the love she and Ryan used to share—so much that she didn't trust herself to look at him now. More than life, she wanted to reach out and squeeze his hand tight, as if just one touch could recapture their past. Last night, had only *she* felt the love?

Nikki got up, turning her hand this way and that, showing off the simple diamond that was sizable without being overpowering.

"Wow!" Christy gasped in awe.

"Beautiful," Joy murmured. Thinking of her own rings, which were tucked away in a jewelry box, she glanced at Ryan's hands. Suddenly she remembered when they'd first touched palms, how strong and wide his hand had felt, how much darker his skin had looked next to hers. Now, at the base of his unadorned ring finger, she could see a tan line where the band had been. Had he continued wearing his wedding ring after he'd gone to California? Maybe, like her, he hadn't removed it until last month, when the divorce was final. She wondered what he'd felt as he put his away. She'd cried.

Christy traipsed over the braided rug, prancing an instant in front of the fire, then lunged and tugged at Joy's pant leg. "Hmm?"

Christy grinned. "Don't you and Daddy have something else for me?"

Ryan pointed toward the tree. "Guess so, since there're still packages."

Coyly crossing her arms, Christy surveyed them, her green eyes sparkling and urgent, her lips twitching in a barely suppressed smile. "You know what I mean."

Joy didn't have a clue. She frowned. Lifting her mug from an end table, she took another sip of hot cider and said, "What?"

Christy rolled her eyes. "You and Daddy are getting married, too. Right?"

Taken aback, Joy darted a glance at Ryan, who looked equally surprised. "We...just came here to get you, Christy."

"You..." The color drained from Christy's face,

and the sparkle was extinguished from eyes that now looked positively wounded.

Joy's voice caught, "Oh, Christmas..."

"Don't call me that!" Bright tears glossed Christy's eyes. "Santa promised me he'd get you and Dad married again. And if Santa backed out, then I don't want to be named Christmas anymore."

Ryan draped his hand along the sofa back, sighing deeply. "Christy, please..."

Nikki saved the day. Loudly clapping her hands, she hopped up. "C'mon, hon," she began, starting in with chatter Joy barely heard. Thankfully Nikki had a way with kids and somehow, it worked. "C'mon, I need your help," Nikki continued. "Jon's opening his gifts from me, and I want you to watch."

"That'll look great on you," Joy said a moment later, taking in the sage sweater that matched Jon's eyes.

Jon was already poking through a box of smaller items. "I can't believe it," he said. "The new version of Windows. And WordPerfect. Pencils. Pads of paper..."

Softly Nikki said, "I thought it was time you got back to writing books, Sleet."

"Lord, you're a pushy woman," Jon rejoined, though the twinkle in his eyes said he didn't mind a bit.

Joy's heart skipped a beat. He was going to write again? Her lips parted, but she couldn't take the opening. Damn Melinda and her constant drive to railroad Jon Sleet into writing again, she suddenly fumed with a venom that surprised her. Having witnessed the newfound love in the man's private life, Joy felt as bad about coming here on business as she did about what Ryan was doing to the Scudders. What had become of her and Ryan, anyway? she ruminated. Eight years ago, they'd been two lower-middle-class kids with love, dreams and ideals. No more; they were fully grown. And now Joy reminded herself that she *did* desperately need her job if she was going to support another child.

When Jon glanced up from the writing supplies, he solved the dilemma by saying, "Well, Joy, since you're here, I might as well ask if SWM would be willing take a look at another children's book."

"Of course. You know they're—*we're,*" she stated, "hot to publish you." Guilty color tinged Joy's cheeks. What she'd wanted had been delivered into her hands without her even working for it, and she didn't even have the nerve to tell Jon she was unemployed. Even worse, Jon assumed, as Ryan had, that Joy had come here for Christy. Lord, she hadn't even known her own daughter was missing!

Christy jumped up and down in the new sneakers, saying, "Are you going to let Mommy publish the story about me, Jon? You know, the one about the man whose touch turns everything to ice until he meets a little girl named Christmas who makes him melt?"

Jon chuckled. "You like that story, huh, Christy?"

"Oh, yeah!"

As Christy skipped toward the tree and began playing with a new Giga pet, Jon briefly outlined the story for Joy. Apparently he'd awakened early this morning and typed it out, which meant Joy could take it back to New York with her. "Since it's another children's book," Jon said, finishing, "it's short. Less than a half hour read."

"Terrific," Joy said, deciding to wait until Christy left the room to tell Jon she'd been fired, since Christy would worry.

Ryan was nestled back in the sofa, surveying her over the rim of his cider mug. "Mission accomplished," he whispered so that no one else could hear. "Guess this means you'll be working for Melinda again."

"Guess that'll be about the time you sign over the Scudders' property to a strip-mall developer," Joy whispered back.

As if on cue, a rap sounded on the door frame and Hub Scudder strode into the room, his hands shoved into the pockets of a flannel-lined jeans jacket he was wearing over stiff, new overalls. "Knocked a bunch on the front door," he said after declining Nikki's offer of coffee. "And I can't stay but a minute. I done saw the sign on the door—"

"The bell's broken," Nikki explained, "and we can't hear the knocker back here, so I put up a sign, so my dad and brothers would know to come on in.''

Hub nodded. ''Well, me 'n Pam figured we'd drive your cab over for you, since it was at the inn, and Jon left the keys in it. Pam's outside, waiting in the truck. Anyhow...'' Hub paused, suddenly looking nervous as his eyes darted to Ryan's. ''I...uh...well, I need to talk to Ryan here.''

So that was the real reason Hub had come. Joy held her breath, feeling hot color returning to her cheeks. Had the Scudders already taken her advice and called Ryan's old boss?

''Yes?'' Ryan listened calmly, his face remaining utterly impassive as Hub explained that under the circumstances he couldn't sell the inn to Ryan.

''You didn't tell me 'n Pam that you turn everything into condos and the like,'' Hub finally said. ''Alls we knew, you was a big city Realtor out in L.A. who could help us.''

Ryan's dark gaze captured Joy's in a penetrating stare before he addressed Hub. ''Well,'' Ryan said, rising from the sofa, ''that's not true anymore. I *worked*—past tense—as a Realtor in L.A. for all of four hours, then I changed my mind and took other employment.''

Hub scratched his head. ''You did?''

Joy's eyes widened. He did?

Ryan nodded. ''See, I've been working in my dad's hardware store, Hub. Anyway, if you'll just come with me...''

Joy watched in amazement as Ryan guided a

hand beneath the elderly man's elbow and began steering him from the room. Standing beside Hub, Ryan looked doubly young and virile, and despite the circumstances, Joy felt slow heat move through her limbs. The mind had no censors, so she immediately thought of the most intimate things they'd done last night. Of Ryan's damp mouth as he suckled her breasts. Of the yearning ache she felt as he slowly, deliciously, caressed between her legs.

Now she could hear his voice fading in the hallway, saying, "I can definitely promise you the inn won't become a mall or a condo. But hell, Hub, I wouldn't be buying it if I didn't have a few plans...."

Joy realized she was staring at her daughter, who was gaping toward the empty doorway. Christy shot Joy a stricken look. "Daddy's building a mall where strippers are gonna dance?" she said with a gasp.

"No, sweetheart," Joy assured. "I thought he might be building a *strip mall*. That's got nothing to do with strippers."

Christy wasn't placated for long. "Well, Daddy did say *hell*," she continued in a chastening voice.

And I'm about to, Joy thought. As in what the *hell* was Ryan up to?

"THANKS AGAIN FOR HELPING me with the last-minute stuff, Joy," Nikki said, hurriedly bringing crystal serving dishes in from a china cabinet.

"I'm just glad there's something I can do." Joy glanced around as she blended whipped cream for the desserts. "And it's definitely easy enough to maneuver in this kitchen." The room was spacious and cheerful—gray, black and red, with gray tile flooring and appliances made for entertaining large groups. It was decorated for Christmas, too; reindeer decanters and a snowman cookie jar were on the counter, and ivy-print dish towels were looped through the handle of the refrigerator door. Outside, snow was falling, but not so fast that Joy couldn't still see Christy's, Jon's and Ryan's footprints in the powder. They'd headed to the barn, so Christy could show her dad the animals.

As she turned off the beater and put away the cream, Joy wished she'd had a chance to talk to Ryan. Was he really working at Holt Hardware? What had happened to his dream job in L.A.? Trying to take her mind off the unanswerable, she said, "You've done so much. You must have been up in the middle of the night cooking."

Nikki chuckled giddily, self-consciously readjusting her new baseball cap by pulling the bill around to the back. "I guess you could say Jon and I were cooking last night."

A rush of wistfulness came behind Joy's answering laughter. Last night, in the wee hours, she and Ryan had been cooking, too. Burning, in fact. Suddenly she blinked, realizing Nikki's eyes were intently fixed on her. "Nikki?"

Nikki swallowed and glanced away. "I..."

Joy caught a dishtowel, quickly drying cream spatters from her hands, her eyebrows knitting with concern. "What?"

"Well…I'm pregnant," Nikki announced in a rush, her cheeks flushing. "I've wanted to tell somebody…"

"Jon?"

"Oh, he knows." Nikki's eyes got misty. "It's not his baby, but he doesn't mind. I wasn't sure how he'd feel about me being pregnant and all, but…"

Leaning against the counter, patting the other woman's arm in support, Joy listened as Nikki told how she'd left home six months ago with a man her father didn't approve of. Nikki had broken off with Buck the day she'd picked up Christy at the airport because Buck didn't want her to have the baby. Nikki swallowed hard. "I know you must think it's terrible to have an unplanned pregnancy…"

Joy quickly shook her head, fighting the urge to divulge her own experience. "No. Things happen." She smiled. "And anyway, you've found Jon."

"I know. And I'm so in love with him. I just wish I'd spoken to my father since I left home."

It was clear she loved her family. Like Joy, she'd lost her mother, and as she talked, Joy realized that Nikki's charming tomboyishness was due to being raised in a rowdy household of boys. Just talking about her estranged father and brothers sent Nikki back into restless action—checking the turkey, the

Jell-O molds, the formal dining room that she and
Joy had set with a lace tablecloth, china and ster-
ling. "I hope my dad likes Jon," Nikki said again,
wringing her hands.

"It would be impossible not to."

"Oh, Joy, that's what I think. And when Dad
finds out that Jon's going to help with the baby…"

Joy squeezed the other woman's hand, then
turned Nikki's palm so the engagement ring was
visible. "Your dad's going to be proud of the match
you've made. Besides, we're all entitled to one mistake."

"I know."

But which was hers? Joy suddenly wondered—
marrying Ryan or divorcing him? Not that marrying
Ryan could have been a mistake when they'd gotten
Christy. No, her mistake was giving up Elayne.

As Nikki turned away, Joy took a deep breath.
Missing Elayne and feeling separated from her aunt
and uncle had made Christmas hard for Joy over
the years. She missed her parents, too. She'd always
sought some quiet time on holidays, to reflect on
the past. Now she glanced at the phone. Should she
call Elayne now? Or wait until after dinner?

"Salad looks great," Nikki said.

With a start, Joy began grating cheese. "About
done, too."

Over her shoulder, Nikki continued, "Please
don't be too mad at Jon for telling Christy you and
Ryan might get back together."

Joy shook her head. "I'm not." Apparently, Jon

had dressed up as Santa last night, and while he'd known better than to make false promises, Christy had caught him off guard in front of the other kids. Joy suddenly chuckled, "Believe me, I know how hard it is to say no to Christy."

"I guess she hoped—"

"She hasn't accepted the divorce yet," Joy explained, training her gaze back on the cheese grater.

Fortunately she didn't have to elaborate, as a booming voice came down the hallway. "Nikki? You there?"

"Dad!"

Nikki whirled around as three pairs of heavy male footsteps tromped closer. And then Nikki was flying across the kitchen and into her dad's open arms.

"Hon," Bruce Ryder said simply, shutting his eyes and hugging Nikki fiercely while the brothers looked on, their eyes glued to their baby sister. Joy couldn't take her eyes from the scene, either, so she barely noticed when Christy, Jon and Ryan came through the kitchen door. No one would ever say the Ryder men were pretty, Joy decided. They were a stout, rough, muscular bunch, clad in jeans and flannel shirts. One had a tattoo on his forearm. Another was wearing a badly battered Stetson. Nevertheless, one thing was certain—to a man, they lived for the one gorgeous female they'd raised after Mrs. Ryder had died.

Joy glanced at Ryan. His cheeks were red from the cold, making his eyes look somehow darker.

Their expression was solemn. Clearly he was as moved by the reunion as she, and when their eyes met, their thoughts seemed to unite for an instant. A fraction of shared hope passed, since reunions were possible, then sadness, since this particular one wasn't theirs. And then the moment was gone. Whatever questions last night's lovemaking had re-opened had somehow been answered in the negative this morning.

Mr. Ryder's booming voice suddenly captured Joy's attention. "Nikki," he said, releasing his daughter, "are you gonna introduce me to the man you're to marry? And should I have brought my shotgun?"

THANKFULLY NO SHOTGUN was needed. For a minute there, Ryan really thought things were heading south fast. Now he said, "Hat's off to you, Nikki. This was great."

"Helluva cook, isn't she?" Bruce Ryder said proudly.

Her three brothers nodded agreement. Bruce Junior, otherwise called Junior, was the oldest. He had a quick sense of humor and wiggled his tattoos in ways that utterly fascinated Christy. "Daddy," Christy had said just moments ago. "Could I get a tattoo for Christmas, since Christmas isn't over yet?"

"What kind of tattoo would you like?" he'd asked.

She'd giggled. "A boy in a bikini. Since Junior's got a girl."

All the adults had howled with laughter. Now Ryan took in the middle, Stetson-wearing brother. Matt, a trucker, had turned out to be the only Ryder with blue rather than brown eyes, and the youngest, nicknamed Skinny, had grown into the brawniest of the four men. Like Nikki, they were all talkers, quick with a joke.

As Ryan finished the last bites of turkey, he found himself missing Joy all over again. Men could never pull together a spread such as this. Patterned cloth napkins matched the edging of the china plates, and candles flickered bringing warmth into the gray winter's afternoon. Everybody looked happy and full.

"Best dressing I ever ate," Jon was saying.

"When Jon and Nikki get married," Christy suddenly piped in, "maybe it could be a double wedding, like I saw some people have on TV."

Ryan's spirits fell. He should have known the meal wouldn't pass without event. "Christy," he said softly, leaning toward where she was seated beside him, feeling conscious of Joy's eyes on his face. "Your mom and I love you, no matter what. But we need to be apart right now."

Christy's chin only shot into the air, as if she didn't believe a word of it. "The wedding could be at the inn," she continued in a wounded, weedling tone. "Mr. and Mrs. Scudder wouldn't mind, and I could be a flower girl."

This time, Ryan's voice carried a warning. "Christy."

"Mom's already got a diamond ring," Christy prompted.

As if buying Joy another ring was what kept them apart. Bringing the napkin from his lap, Ryan laid it beside his plate. He was forming his answer when he realized the room had gone dead silent. Glancing up, Ryan's gaze followed everyone else's to the doorway—and landed on a girl he barely recognized.

Joy was merely staring, her skin pale, her bright red mouth slack and her eyes wide with surprise. When she spoke, her voice was strangely strangled. "Elayne?"

The thirteen-year-old glared back, looking like a younger, more insolent, long-haired version of Joy. Her hair was white-blond and wavy, like Christy's, but so long that one toss of her head sent it cascading over her shoulder. Otherwise, Elayne didn't move. She dropped an army-style, fatigue-green duffel on the floor, then she just stood there with a navy pea coat thrown over her shoulder, hooked by a finger, and her other hand shoved into the back pocket of tight black jeans. A small hoop earring was affixed to one of her sparse blond eyebrows, but not even the defiant jewelry and murderous expression could obscure that she was growing up. She had a budding woman's body, one she obviously wasn't quite comfortable with yet. That alone made Ryan's heart go out to her, and he felt a sudden urge to protect his niece in this room of big, brawny men. Not that she noticed. She was staring at Joy. And with more temper than Ryan himself could muster on a bad day.

"Elayne?" Joy said again, almost in a whisper.

And then Elayne said the most surprising thing. Her voice dripping with sarcasm, she said, "What, *Mother?*" Turning, she stared at Ryan. "Like, uh," she began, "you *did* know she wasn't really my aunt, right? But then, maybe she didn't bother to clue you in. 'Cause, Uncle Ryan, she sure as hell didn't bother mentioning it to me."

Chapter Six

"Elayne?" Joy croaked again, slowly rising, uncertainly clutching the napkin from her lap, staring into emerald eyes so much like her own that she could have been looking into a mirror. The sun, which had been visible through the window, vanished behind clouds and eclipsed the room, and flames from the candles flickered as if pushed by the winds driving down the quickening snow.

Vaguely Joy registered that these weren't good omens. And as always, when she looked at Elayne, everything else receded. From seemingly far off, she heard ice rattle in a goblet, then she felt, rather than saw, Christy's head tilt in puzzlement at an almost comical angle, and how Ryan had tensed, the way he always did before he screamed bloody murder.

Only a second had passed.

Joy managed to clear her throat. "Elayne, how did you..."

"Find out you got rid of me?"

At the caustic words, Joy impulsively stepped

forward, hand outstretched. But even if Elayne
hadn't made such a point of shrinking against the
door frame, the anger blazing in her eyes would
have stayed Joy's steps. Elayne's chin lifted a
prideful notch as if to say Joy wasn't needed. "*Aunt
May* told me before she died." Elayne spat out the
words. "Because *you* didn't have the guts. You'd
never have the guts."

Joy said in a rush, "But that's been over a month
ago…"

"No, *Mother,*" Elayne shot back, imbuing the
word with venom. "Like, uh, let's get this right.
It's not a *month,* 'kay? You've been lying for
years."

Vaguely realizing she'd dropped her napkin, Joy
slid her hand over the back of a dining chair to
steady herself. Despite the circumstances, her eyes
kept moving quickly, hungrily over the child she'd
given birth to and whom she'd so desperately
wanted to know. Emotions overwhelmed her—love
and worry. Grief for their losses. And most important, the thoughts: *Oh, Elayne, my baby! You know
I'm your mother! You know!*

Lord, her daughter was going to be a beauty. But
she was at the worst of awkward ages—getting
breasts, acne, braces. Joy's eyes widened. And earrings? One in her *eyebrow?* Elayne was *thirteen!*
Sally Bower had assured Joy that Elayne was grieving right now, but still well-adjusted…a good kid.

"Like, uh," Elayne began, putting out a hand as
if to stop traffic. "If you've got some problem with

the way I look, chalk it up to lack of maternal input. 'Kay?''

Joy ventured a step around her chair, still studiously ignoring how Ryan teetered at the periphery of her vision. What was he thinking? How was she going to explain? Not that it mattered right now. Joy's firstborn needed explanations more than Ryan did. ''I love the way you look,'' Joy said, focusing on Elayne and the warnings that flashed from the glittering slashes of her eyes. ''I always have. You're beautiful, you're—''

''Just not beautiful enough for you, huh?''

Relaxing her stance, Elayne leaned more casually against the doorjamb, but her studied stance of bored nonchalance couldn't hide how she was hurting, how betrayed she felt. Fighting not to reach out again, Joy told herself doing so would only make matters worse. But pain welled in her chest. She wanted to touch her daughter so much! She'd waited so long! She wanted to hold her so tight that Elayne would feel the depth of her love. When she spoke again it was carefully. ''I didn't get rid of you, Elayne.''

Elayne merely stared.

Fleetingly Joy's eyes darted around, registering Christy's and Ryan's stunned expressions. She didn't want to speak in front of them, but this might be her only chance. ''I was fifteen…''

Elayne glanced down at her fingernails, which Joy noticed were bright red. Elayne snapped, ''Is this supposed to be new information? I mean, like, everybody in Beckley knows!''

"No, they don't." Joy's voice quivered with emotion. She glanced toward Ryan, not meeting his eyes. "Ryan, why don't you take Christy into the other room?"

He didn't move.

Before Joy could ask again, Elayne tossed her head. "Anyway, I went over to Ritts's Computer Land…''

The sudden pain in Elayne's eyes made clear that Doug Ritts had rejected her. "Oh, Elayne," Joy whispered, heartbreak for her daughter threatening to overwhelm her. "Did Mrs. Bower know you went there? Why didn't she—''

"Tell you?" Elayne gaped, pulling a hand from her back pocket and gripping it tightly on the door molding. "Because like, maybe you weren't around!''

Joy suppressed the desire to cast her eyes around the room and make sure the world was still there. She'd become so intent on Elayne that everything else—the china, crystal and silver—had become a glinting blur, leaving only the impression of slanting light and out-of-focus faces. "You told me you didn't want me to come to Beckley," Joy said. "You said you didn't want to come to New York until *after* Christmas.''

"Now you know why.''

Shock was being replaced by other concerns, and

Joy's mind was starting to reel. "Wait a minute. How did you get here, Elayne?"

"As if you care."

Dammit, Elayne was getting the best of her, choking up all Joy's secret doubts. *She's right. I gave her up. I didn't care.* Joy's voice shook with protest. "I do care." *I love you!*

"A plane. That's how I got here."

Joy searched her face. "Do the Bowers know where you are?"

"No."

"What did you use for—"

"Money?" Elayne released a harsh laugh. "Like, duh. You've been generous enough with that, right, *Aunt* Joy? It's everything else you had trouble with."

Joy wanted Elayne to have everything she needed, but now Elayne made it sound so twisted. "I—I would have come if you'd said you wanted me there," Joy ventured. "But you said you wanted to finish the term, to deal with things on your own."

"Right," Elayne snapped back fiercely. "But I can't impose on strangers forever, can I?"

Elayne wasn't imposing, and the Bowers weren't strangers. "Elayne, I want you in New York. I—" Joy's voice cracked. "For years, I've wanted you with me. I—I didn't see more of you because it hurt so much to be near you and not able to...to say were my...my..." Even now, as tears blurred her vision, Joy could barely say it. Maybe because, deep down, she felt she'd given up the right. "My daughter."

Elayne rolled her eyes. "Daughter? Get real."

God, as many times as Joy had practiced some of these words, why were they were coming out all wrong? "I didn't want it to be like this," Joy said. Tears weren't supposed to be gathering in her eyes. Her throat wasn't supposed to be closing up, aching with fire. Strangers weren't supposed to be staring, and Ryan and Christy were supposed to be prepared. "Not…on Christmas day, not like this" was all she managed to get out.

"Well, I never was convenient, was I?"

"Please," Joy said in a strangled whisper. "I was two years older than you are now." She'd barely had breasts, hadn't reached her full height. She'd still been spending hours in front of the mirror treating blemishes. One infinitesimal red spot, and she'd want to hide for a week.

Fifteen when she'd conceived. Not old enough to have a baby.

Understanding appeared then vanished from Elayne's eyes, and was replaced by contempt.

"I wasn't ready to take care of a baby, Elayne."

"Just ready to make one, huh?"

It was the charge Joy secretly leveled at herself. Her hand slid off the dining chair, reaching for something more solid. As she gripped the table's edge, the rough feel of the lace on her palm was somehow jarring. Fine, delicate things weren't supposed to be rough—not lace, not parenthood. "I'd lost my parents that year. I was...lonely, frightened, confused.''

''Of course.'' Elayne's head bobbed up and down, making her long blond waves dance in the dark candlelight. ''How else could I have been conceived?''

''That's not what I meant! Please don't twist this around, Elayne. We're all we've got—''

''If you're all I've got, I'm in big trouble.''

''Please,'' Joy said again, her voice tremulous. ''I'd lived with Aunt May and Uncle Jer. Elayne, I knew how good they were with kids. They loved you so much.''

Elayne's chin trembled, and she clamped her mouth shut to stop it. ''More than you, that's for sure.''

''No, not *more* than me!'' Joy burst out, her hand that gripped the tablecloth tightening, drawing her plate closer to the table's edge. ''Just differently. I was desperate for you to have a life. Two parents. A future, an education, a career—''

''Aren't you talking about *you?*''

''What?''

''You ditched me and went to Paris.''

''I wanted what was best for you.'' Joy's voice gentled, catching with years of suppressed heartache. ''I thought I could know you, Elayne. That I could watch you grow since I wasn't giving you to strangers. But it hurt so much when I saw you.

When I heard you call me your aunt...when you wanted May to hold you, not me..."

How could she ever explain the heartache? "I love you, Elayne. I always have. I always will."

As a tear splashed down Elayne's cheek, she swiped at it with an angry brush of her hand. "I hate you." Suddenly ducking, she grabbed her duffel, then whirled around and ran down the hallway.

Joy bolted after her. "Elayne!"

Elayne's footsteps pounded toward a staircase. "Leave me alone!"

Only the fact that Elayne had come here kept Joy going. Elayne wanted a family. Wanted Joy. Otherwise she'd never have come. But she'd lost May and Jer, had obviously been rejected by her father and she felt Joy had betrayed her. *You did betray her.* Giving her up had felt right at the time, but later...

"Elayne, please. I'm begging you. Stop."

"Stay away!"

Breathless, Joy stopped, expecting—but not hearing—Ryan's footsteps behind her. Resting her hand on the newel post, she listened as Elayne continued upstairs in a house she'd never even visited. A stranger's house. Joy's heart squeezed, aching with the inappropriateness of it. Why hadn't May told Joy she intended to tell Elayne the truth? Well, maybe May hadn't known. Who could imagine the last moments of life when the burning need came to unburden oneself and set things right?

"I'll just give her a few minutes," Joy whispered. Feeling weak, as if her insides had been taken out and shaken, Joy headed toward the dining room. For the first time, she took a good look at Ryan. His expression still dangerously blank. Lovely. He was definitely about to blow. Which, Joy reminded herself, was one reason they were divorced. So often in their marriage, he'd flown off the handle when she'd needed support. Christy was squinting, looking perplexed, but not unduly disturbed. Jon Sleet and the Ryders were silently studying their empty plates. Joy didn't blame them one bit.

"Don't mind me," she said as she headed for the opposite door that led to the kitchen. "I've got to call the Bowers. They're probably worried sick."

In the kitchen, she lifted the phone receiver. For a moment, she merely clutched it over her still-pounding heart. Her whole world had just been rearranged, and it felt good—damn good—to hold onto something solid.

Especially when she heard Ryan enter the room.

"GO AHEAD," Joy murmured after she'd said goodbye to Sally. "Yell and scream at me."

"No," Ryan said simply. Gently lifting the phone receiver from her hand, he quietly eased it into the cradle. He could feel her waiting for his burst of temper—the one he knew wasn't going to come. Not this time. Calmly he turned away from where she'd leaned beside him at the kitchen counter, just long enough to pour two cups of coffee. He was aware of her hands, flitting nervously over the gray countertop, moving a cheese grater and egg beater into the sink.

Her voice suddenly caught. "You're sure I shouldn't go after Elayne?"

He shook his head, stirring in the amount of sugar Joy used to take. "I just talked to her. She needs a minute."

"Christy?"

"She's fine. She's with Nikki."

"Thanks." Joy traced the handle of the steaming coffee mug he slid toward her, but she didn't lift it. Her voice shook. "I mean it, Ryan. Thanks."

As much as for help with the kids, she was thanking him for not letting his confused emotions surface as anger. "I wanted to yell," he found himself admitting in measured tones. Hell, for years, he'd blown like a skyrocket at the least provocation. And when he'd heard the exchange in the dining room…

Before he could continue, Joy said, her voice full of concern, "What's this about you working for your dad?"

As if his secrets were anywhere near as mind-shattering as hers. Turning the focus to him was so typically Joy that he allowed himself a sigh of frustration. "Yeah, I am," he returned, still taking in the nervous movements of her hands as she fiddled with the mug handle. After a moment, he glanced through the window since he wasn't sure what he wanted to say next.

Deep breath.

Joy had taken them for years. And in the last eight months, a woman named Laura had taught Ryan how to. "You don't have to react," Laura always said. "Not immediately, Ryan. Besides words can hurt. And sometimes you don't get a second chance to say what you mean, so take it easy. Think carefully before you speak." *And then maybe you won't leave your wife for a job you don't even want. Maybe then she'll trust you not to yell when you find out her niece is really her daughter.*

Exhaling slowly, Ryan gazed at the sloping snow-blanketed hills outside, then at the barn and forest beyond. The wind had picked up and turned westerly; it was snowing harder. After a second, Ryan's eyes settled on a fountain that Jon and Christy had shown him not two hours ago—bronzed figures inside a knee-high stone enclosure.

Joy's voice was tentative as she edged closer. "I didn't realize you…left the job in L.A."

His dark eyes settled on her lighter ones. Tilting his head, he kept his voice gentle, but it caught with all the emotion he was trying to process. "Seems like there's a lot we didn't realize, Joy."

She swallowed visibly, and the fast-ticking pulse in her throat assured him she knew he'd been referencing her relationship to Elayne. She said, "I know how badly you wanted that job."

How long was she going to push him to talk about himself—when *her* life and *her* feelings should be the focus now? He almost wished she was intentionally avoiding the issues. But he knew Joy was simply—as always—putting everybody else first. Didn't she understand that he was tired of talking about himself? That he actually wanted to know about *her?*

Not that he would withhold the information she wanted. She needed answers. Blowing out another sigh, he set down his coffee mug, shoved his hands deep into his jeans pockets and surveyed her. "Joy, I never even wanted that job. When I told you about it, it was nothing more than an offer."

She looked stunned. "You hadn't accepted it?"

"No. But the way you responded...I realized how much we'd grown apart. How hard things had gotten between us. How we weren't really..."

...in love anymore.

He might as well have said it aloud. Joy glanced away, biting her lower lip to keep it from trembling. For an instant, her eyes darted toward the doorway as if Elayne might appear, then her gaze met his again. "There's so much we don't know about each other," she said shakily. "Your life in L.A. isn't what I thought. And Laura..."

He squinted. "Laura?"

Heightened color spread on her cheeks. "Once Christy tried to call, but your mother said you were gone for the evening, at Laura's."

He offered a short, rueful laugh. "And Christy didn't tell you who Laura was?"

"No."

He shrugged. "I guess she was trying to protect me."

Color was still flooding Joy's face, turning it crimson. "Your life requires no more explanation than mine. We're divorced, Ryan. I didn't mean to imply I have any right to—"

"Joy." Now she couldn't even look at him. Quickly, he cupped her chin, lifting it, and his eyes lasered into hers. "I told you last night there'd been no one. I hadn't been with a woman since we last shared a bed." Unmistakable huskiness came into his voice, lowering it. "I've *never* been with another women. I've done a lot of things Joy, but last night I wasn't lying. I've never lied to you."

Joy looked as if she'd rather be anywhere than here, even though gentle, sensuous heat was softening her gaze. Suddenly he was conscious of her body—her physical warmth, her soft red lips that even in these unlikely circumstances he suddenly, desperately, wanted to possess...to nip and suck, for comfort and for the remembrance of the past. And maybe because it was easier when words were failing him.

"Well..." Her chin trembled just once, but violently, beneath his thumb's caress. "Who is she?"

"Laura is my therapist."

Joy's eyes widened. "Your *what!*"

Looking away, letting his hand drop, he felt an unwanted and very uncharacteristic heat in his own cheeks. It wasn't easy for him to admit he'd gone to see someone. But maybe he needed to lay it all

on the line for Joy. What if there were no more
opportunities? Divorced or not, *he* still felt Joy had
a right to ask about other woman. And he definitely
wanted more information about what he'd heard in
the dining room.

Deep breath.

Raising his gaze to hers again, he felt as if his
heart was twisting inside his chest. It looped and
knotted, leaving him feeling confused and breathless. And all because his wife was so pretty, with
her fair poreless skin and eyes so sparkling green.
Lifting a hand, he glided his fingers around her
nape and up, into short hair that looked nearly plat-
inum in this light. Strands gathered in the grooves
between his fingers, like silk yarns at a loom, and
they were so unimaginably soft that his groin tightened. Oh, dammit, of all the times to react to her,
to get hard. He couldn't believe it. He let his hand
drift away again, but otherwise edged along the
counter, coming closer.

"When I left New York..." *Left you and
Christy.* "I knew it was over, Joy. But I kept wondering what went wrong. What I could have done.
Our lives had gotten so out of control. I was always
working, flying off at the handle. You were spread
too thin, trying to be the perfect mom and having
a career of your own..."

She still looked positively shocked. "So you
went to a *therapist?*"

"Not a very Ryan Holt thing to do, huh?" His
lips lifted in a smile that didn't reach his eyes. He

was so anxious to find out about her, but he knew how Joy operated. It was everybody else first. "I learned a lot about us, about me. I just..." He glanced away for a moment. "Had to simplify my life, you know?"

She nodded. "Yeah. I wish I could do that."

You can, Joy. But only if you want it bad enough. "The reason the checks I've sent for Christy are printed with my parents' address is because I'm living there. At first, I got an apartment over in Santa Monica. It was splashy, with great views, but so empty..." He sighed. "You know the kind of place. Anyway, the second I moved in, I realized it was all wrong." He paused. "My *life* was all wrong. So, I went home. I started sleeping in the room I used to share with Tom and helping dad in the store. I guess I needed to get back to...to the way things used to be. When I still didn't feel completely right, I started seeing Laura."

Which was why he knew he'd been at least half the problem in his and Joy's marriage. He was too much of a taker, and he had an anger problem. But they'd never make it unless she changed, too. Laura said he couldn't tell Joy that, either. She had to discover it herself. Most probably, she never would.

"You did that for us?"

He wanted to say yes, but was honest. "Not really, Joy. At first, I did it for me." *The way I always did everything for me.* "Everything was gone—you, Christy. The marriage was over. I'd walked out. But face it, you didn't want me there. I...I started seeing Laura because I hated the man I'd become.''

Unshed tears made Joy's eyes sparkle like gemstones as she laid a hand tentatively on his forearm. ''Ryan, I used to try to remember the first time you weren't there when I needed you. Or when you needed me and I felt so resentful that I didn't bother to show up.''

His voice was tight, his heart pounding harder than he wanted. ''Me, too.''

A slight catch turned her voice throaty. ''When did we quit being good to each other?''

When we started always talking about me, Joy, and never you. When you wanted to please me so much that you quit being honest—with both me and with yourself—about what you wanted and needed from me. Oh, baby, you didn't even know you were doing it.

He felt suddenly driven to reach out to the woman beside him. Nearly nine years ago they'd stood at the altar saying, ''I do.'' Nearly nine years! Knowing he shouldn't, he allowed himself just one more touch—a long trailing brush of a thumb that crossed her cheek and stilled at the corner of her mouth. Raising his gaze from her parting lips, he slowly shook his head, looking more deeply into her eyes than he ever had in all the years they'd been together. ''Joy,'' he said, with wrenching tenderness in his voice. ''I am *so* sorry.''

''Sorry?''

He nodded. ''Yeah. Sorry I didn't listen better.

And that…that I never really knew you." Even now, he could barely believe his wife had had a whole other life, a secret hidden past of which he'd known nothing. How could he begin to process what had happened in the dining room? He'd gone after Elayne and found her in Jon's study, a dark room, somber with wood paneling, heavy furniture and shelves crammed with books. She'd been staring out a window at the falling snow, her back turned.

"You need to talk," he'd said simply, in a way he never could have before his sessions with Laura.

Elayne hadn't looked nearly as tough as she had downstairs, so he'd ventured closer, gently lifting her coat from the floor where she'd thrown it and setting it atop a desk. "One thing I know about Joy," he'd continued gently, "is that she's always looking out for other people. She's always trying to do what she thinks they want her to do, or what's best."

"And she can decide what's best for me?"

His heart pulling, he'd rested a hand on Elayne's shoulder. "Joy and I never talked about this, Elayne. But downstairs, she said she was young. And you were a baby."

"Well, I'm not a baby now."

"No." He turned her slowly to face him. "You're not. But you're not alone, either, Elayne. You've got family."

"You're not my family anymore, Uncle Ryan," she'd said, her eyes cloudy with tears. "You're di-

vorced. And anyway, you're not even really related.''

"Blood doesn't matter," he'd said levelly, trying
to communicate the truth of it with a steady gaze.
"I don't give a care about blood. We're related by
marriage. And what matters to me is you, Elayne."
When her tears fell, he proved his love by hauling
her to his chest and wrapping her in his arms.

"Oh, Uncle Ryan," she shuddered, dropping her
defiant tone. "If I've got no place to go…"

"As long as I'm around," he'd assured, "you've
got a place. And Joy wants you with her. She really
does." As Elayne's arms tightened around his mid-
section, Ryan wondered how he'd lived so long,
feeling so cut off from his emotions. All those
years, he'd been on the hamster wheel—running to
the next job, the next deal. Lord, Laura was right.
Ryan might have accomplished a lot, but he hadn't
felt—really felt—anywhere near the range of possible human emotions.

Well, Ryan Holt was sure feeling now.

"I never even knew you," he murmured to Joy
again, still staring deeply into her eyes. "I wish
you'd told me…" Suddenly, he shut his eyes. *Deep
breath,* he thought. *Deep, deep breath. Exhale,
Ryan.* "And Christmases," he said, looking into her
eyes again. "When I'd find you alone…"

Joy's voice was strangled. "I've always taken
time on holidays, to think about her for a while."

Not knowing what to do, Ryan helplessly rested
his hands on Joy's shoulders. Slowly he skimmed

them down to her elbows, then back up again, his palms smoothing the sleeves of her black blazer as if to warm her.

She said, "I can't believe you're not mad at me."

He knew better than to say it, but couldn't stop himself. "Even now, you're worried about me. And Elayne. But what about *you,* Joy? Are *you* okay?"

"Fine." But of course she wasn't. "And you're *sure* you're not..."

"Mad?" He shook his head. "No." Not that he blamed her for thinking he would be. "Eight months ago, I would have been. I would have been hurt because you'd kept secrets. Now I know you probably would have told me things, if only I'd taken more time to listen."

"Don't be hard on yourself," Joy said quickly, trailing an arm along the countertop, as if to brace herself. "You were just busy. Work was so stressful."

For the first time today, real anger sparked inside him. "Quit making excuses for me," he growled. Immediately gentling his tone, he added, "Please, Joy."

Her eyes widened. "Sorry."

And don't apologize. Dammit, Joy, for once, just tell me I was lousy to live with. Before he could speak, Joy said, "I was so confused when it happened."

Putting aside his anger and simply opening his heart, Ryan listened—really listened to her as he never had before—while she told him the story of how she'd come to let her aunt and uncle raise Elayne. "And now, nothing I do is going to make it right, Ryan."

"Well, I know how to do one thing right, anyway," he found himself saying thickly, unexpectedly reaching for her, suddenly not giving a damn about the consequences. He didn't expect her to come so easily, to yield against his chest. Tightening his strong forearms around her back, he breathed a hum of comfort into her hair. He was barely aware of her body—of her skin's sweet scent and her the fine blond strands of silken hair that caught on his lips. Oh, he knew she was warm and shapely, soft where he was hard—and turning hot, just the way she'd always turned hot for him. But mostly, the sheer ache of her heart was touching the sheer ache of his. He swept his mouth back and forth across her forehead, as if a few feathery, not-quite-kisses could actually smooth the wrinkles of her worried frown.

He suddenly groaned. "And the way I berated you for spending too much money…"

Joy gazed up at him. "I was putting some away," she admitted. "So Elayne can go to college if she doesn't get a scholarship. You know, Aunt May didn't have much. There was Uncle Jer's life insurance, and now, of course, with May's policy and the house…"

He should have guessed sooner. "You were putting away money for Elayne."

Her cheek rubbed his shoulder as she nodded. "I've always wanted her to have opportunities. Especially for college." In the hitch of Joy's voice he could hear what she left unsaid, that her own scholarships had helped allow her a life other than that of teenage motherhood. "And I did want to tell you, Ryan. Sometimes, I'd have fantasies that she'd come to live with us. But we were in college, and then Christy was born. At first, we could barely support ourselves, and we were both working so much. By the time it was really feasible, Elayne was older. By then, she thought May and Jer were her parents, and she was so happy."

"When we met, was it..." He could barely get out the words he was murmuring against her hair. "Was it really so hard to talk to me, Joy?"

"Oh, no—" Leaning back a fraction, she looked at him, her eyes warming. "I could have told you anything, but I was so afraid of losing you, Ryan. I didn't think you'd walk away. But then, every time I'd start to tell you, I'd think 'what if, what if, what if...'" She exhaled a shaky sigh, reaching to touch his cheek. "You'll never know what you meant to me."

"I know—" His voice was thick again as he caught her hand, cradling her fingers against his cheek. "I know because I felt it, too, Joy."

And he still did. Because something deep inside him was shaking loose right now. He thought he'd known everything about this woman. He knew how dangerous she looked when suppressing her anger, how airy she sounded when she giggled. But more than that, he'd *had* her. Lain beside her in a beam of sunlight, entering her while golden rays played on the sparse glistening ginger curls between her legs. Intimately he'd thrust his fingers between the lips of her mouth so she could suckle as he filled her. He knew what she looked like, nervous and naked, kneeling down in front of him. Knew exactly how the silk of her palms felt, sliding slowly down his thighs as her hot tongue flickered out, caressing the hard length of him. How many times had this woman pulled him over the edge, quivering and shuddering, bursting with ecstasy?

Oh, yeah, he'd definitely known everything. Or so he'd thought.

Now guilt twisted inside him. "I should have asked you more questions. I never should have pushed you to spend time with May and Jer."

Lifting a hand, she pressed a finger to his lips. "But you were right, Ryan. I should have. I wish I had. I loved them so much and, after my parents died, they were all I had left. But the situation just—" she shrugged helplessly "—got out of control for all of us."

What a tragedy. Who could have anticipated the problems the family had faced? he wondered. And then another truth hit him. Venomous jealousy surfaced but was quickly submerged, leaving dull hurt in its place. *I wasn't the only one.* "You were with another man."

He could see her throat work as she swallowed. "Once. And he was a boy."

It shouldn't have hurt so much. Not that Ryan was really getting angry. It was just…just…

Oh, hell. He suddenly felt more helpless than a man should. Not even Laura could have prepared him for this. His voice was low, raw. "Damn, Joy," he said, allowing himself one curse as he ran a hand through his hair, pushing the dark strands back, off his face, the gesture somehow calming him. "I thought you were a virgin. All that time, I thought I was the only man you'd ever—"

"You *were.*" Her eyes were wet now, glossy with tears, but she wasn't crying; her gaze stayed steadier than he'd ever seen it. "You *are* the only man, Ryan."

Unwanted hope had lodged in his throat. "I am?"

As she nodded, he felt the last vestiges of their childhood slipping away. He'd never realized that it was leaving them all these years. But now it was gone. Forever. He and Joy weren't young lovers anymore, or struggling students, or yuppies treading on a hamster wheel.

He was a man.

She was a woman.

"You were the only boy who mattered, Ryan. And I know I shouldn't say this, but sometimes I think you'll be the only man. I…" Her voice trailed off and she glanced away. "When I try to imagine being with someone else…"

The thought hurt. "You try to imagine?"

"Yeah, because I'm trying so hard to get over you. I shut my eyes…" She reached, took his hand, and brought it to her heart. "I feel his hands…"

"And?"

"And his face is always yours."

He didn't even question the relief he felt. His hand slid beneath the lapel of her jacket, over her soft wool sweater, grazing her collarbone and resting on her shoulder. He shook his head. "I can't believe how little I know about you, Joy. What did we say to each other all those years?"

"I don't know," she returned as he rubbed a thumb along her neck. "I can't believe you're back at home. And with Ma and Pop." Wistfulness touched her voice. Last night, after they made love, she'd asked about his parents, and he knew she missed them. "So," she continued, "I guess I don't really know you, either." Her eyes asked what her lips didn't dare. *Is there any chance for us?*

He answered aloud, honestly. "I don't know." After a moment, a slight smile lifted the corners of his lips. "Deep sigh," he whispered.

Her gaze still held concern for Elayne, but Joy managed a small smile. Inhaling a deep breath, she audibly exhaled. "Deep sigh," she echoed.

"Whatever happens, I want you to know I'll do anything I can to help you with Elayne. All the money I made in New York is invested, and my expenses are low because I'm at Ma and Pop's, so if you need—"

"No, really. I…"

Her voice trailed off, and suddenly, he was hit with another wave of emotion. He couldn't live without her. He had been in denial, spent eight months on a therapist's couch, hoping Laura could show him how to let go. But he needed Joy more than ever, and as always, the expression of that need came, in part, as physical want. With his eyes settling on her small red mouth, he craved the feel of it. He wanted to probe the soft warmth that belonged to him—only to him. Marriage had made Joy too much a part of him to ever let go. She was in his soul, his blood.

But all their relationships were changing so fast; they weren't the same people they'd been eight months ago. Or even ten minutes ago. He and Joy were divorced. Elayne was a daughter, not a niece. They no longer hid the same secrets. Or carried lies in their hearts. And because even the simplest kiss would be so explosive, Ryan only said, "Just know I'm here. I'm willing."

"You can't know how much it means."

But he did. He smiled. "Let's go find Elayne and Christy. We'll sit down and have a talk."

"You don't mind?"

Even the gratitude in her voice somehow hurt. Didn't she know he'd still do anything in the world for her? He gazed into her face a long moment, feeling the responding touch of her eyes—how they flickered over his dark hair with longing, then searched his face. Suddenly tears brightened her eyes.

"C'mon, now," he said gently. "Don't cry, Joy-to-the-world."

"You might not be my husband anymore—" She paused, blinking back the moisture. "But you're still the best."

"You always had faith in me." Draping an arm around her shoulders, he felt hers snake around his waist. "C'mon."

Just as they turned toward the interior door, Nikki burst in from the hallway, a leather bomber jacket open, her new mirrored baseball cap in hand and her cheeks ruddy. "Have you seen Christy and Elayne?" she gasped. "I—" Cutting herself off, Nikki raised her voice, shouting. "Jon? Hon? Can you hear me?"

"Yeah?" Jon yelled from another room.

Nikki's voice leaped with worry. "Have you seen Christy and Elayne? Dad, have you? I thought they were in the barn. But they're gone. So is one of the horses. And I found this." Nikki held up a small white glove.

Joy gasped. "It's Christy's."

Nikki nodded. "Well, I think they're gone."

Joy's hand clamped harder on Ryan's waist, feeling like ice through his shirt. "Gone?" she repeated.

"Gone," Nikki affirmed. "I think they ran away."

Chapter Seven

"You can't take Jon's horse without asking because that's stealing," Christy called with certainty. Squinting against the blowing, blinding snow, she kept pushing through the drifts—avoiding the worst, which were waist-high, but often sinking to her knees as she tried to catch Elayne, but Elayne was moving too fast, holding the reins and guiding King. Staring at her receding back, Christy wailed, "Wait, Elayne!"

Elayne didn't even turn around.

Grunting with effort, Christy clumsily ran after her sister, but it was too difficult. The adult-size rubber boots she'd pulled on over the platform sneakers kept tripping her, and her calves were aching with the steep climb. Raising her voice, Christy demanded, "Are you gonna ride King or what?"

Elayne's annoyed words whisked back to Christy on the fierce wind. "Go back, Christy! What I'm doing is none of your business!"

"Is, too." A sudden shiver made Christy wish she was wearing something warmer than a parka that had been Jon's daughter's. Because the sleeves were too short, an inch of red exposed skin ringed her wrist between glove and sleeve—at least on the hand where she *had* a glove. She'd lost one. Shoving both hands deep into pockets, she bravely told herself she didn't even care if she froze to death. She just wanted information. "Are you really my sister or what?" When that didn't work, she shrieked, *"Ma soeur?"*

Tugging the reins, Elayne ignored her and continued urging King to climb higher, into the woods. As they wound through the snow-heavy trees, the shadows deepened.

"Well, are you?" Christy shivered again. "Elayne!"

As Elayne whirled around, long blond waves whipped across her cheeks; her eyes were blazing mad. She just stood there, gripping King's reins until Christy reached her, then she yelled, "I mean it! Go back to the barn!"

When Elayne started walking again, Christy wrenched around and realized the barn was out of sight. They were deep in the darkening woods. She was lost! And Elayne hated her! "Wait! You can't leave me here, Elayne!"

Christy tried to run, her short legs plowing through the knee-high snow. "What was my mom talking about?" she shrieked. Christy should have asked her mom what she meant in the dining room, but her mom might have said it was grown-up talk. "Tell me, Elayne! What did it mean?"

Elayne stopped in her tracks, then very slowly turned around. "Like, duh. Are you stupid or what? It means your mother's a liar. She had me, just like she had you, but she didn't want to raise me, so she dumped me on Aunt May and Uncle Jer and went to Paris."

Christy pulled up short a few paces from Elayne, suddenly afraid to go closer because Elayne was so hateful. "My mom's not mean."

"Your mom's a *bitch*, Christy."

Christy rapidly fluttered her eyelids, fighting tears and the wind. When she opened her mouth to speak, hair blew into her face, catching on her lips. "If my mom was a..." She stopped, swallowing hard because she'd never cursed out loud before. "A *b-i-t-c-h*," she defensively spelled out, "she didn't mean it."

Elayne's face set. "Get lost, you idiot!"

Her heart pounding with panic, Christy stared as Elayne turned her back once more. "You're the idiot!" Christy burst out, the frigid breath she drew making her lungs burn. "You're the one who's mean! And earrings aren't s'posed to go in your eyebrows!" Afraid she'd sob, Christy clamped her mouth shut a second, then said, "I didn't even *want* a sister, anyway!"

Elayne's shoulders sagged with annoyance. "Good," she shouted over her shoulder. "Because I didn't ask to be one."

Christy's chin quivered. Elayne was really missing out, because Christy would have been a great little sister. She was sure of it. "My teacher, Mrs. Konroy, says I'm popular," she yelled as a warm tear rolled down her cheek. "Other people like me!"

"Whatever."

Christy kept following, but more cautiously, since Elayne didn't want her to. As they broke through a clearing, she watched Elayne guide King beside a tree stump. Using it as a stepping stone, Elayne shoved a toe into a stirrup, then hoisted herself into the saddle.

No! Christy's heart stuttered. Was Elayne really leaving her? She couldn't leave if they were supposed to be sisters, could she? Panicking, Christy spun around. The barn was gone! So was Jon's house! Dark woods were everywhere; snow, bushes, trees and fallen logs lay in every direction. Wildly Christy ran, lurching toward Elayne and the horse. "Elayne, don't leave!"

"Stay back, Christy!"

But already, Christy's panicked voice had made the horse rear. Long muscular legs wildly pawing the air right above her head. Gasping, staring straight up, Christy listened to Elayne's labored grunt and watched her sister twist, fighting with the reins. Wide-eyed, Christy craned her head so far back she nearly fell, and held her breath as the hooves crashed down, narrowly missing her and spraying snow.

"Look what you've done!" Elayne cried.

"I didn't do anything!"

"You could have been killed!"

"I bet you'd like that!" Christy's bulging eyes were still so full of frightened tears that Elayne was a blur on the big horse. Becoming conscious of the freezing wind again, Christy realized that her rubber boots were nearly buried in the snow. "You can't leave me here," she repeated, her voice shaking as another tear fell.

Elayne looked close to tears herself. "Why did you have to follow me?"

Christy's lips stretched thin, as she held back a sob. Her sister would hate her even more if she cried. "If you're gonna run away," she said, controlling herself, "then you have to take me."

"Why?"

"'Cause last night Santa promised me he was getting Mom and Dad back together, but he didn't do it, so now I want to run away, too." Besides, Christy had run away last week, and she had experience. King skittered sideways, making Christy shuffle quickly back. Tripping, she fell on her behind, then scrambled up from the snow.

Not that Elayne cared. "There's no such thing as Santa Claus," she said, pointing into the distance. "And the barn's that way."

Christy whirled around, half expecting to see the barn. Maybe when she looked before, she just hadn't noticed. But no, it was still gone. And now Elayne was really leaving! "No!" Christy cried, watching her sister expertly tug the reins, her body turning in tandem with King's.

"Giddy up!" Elayne kicked King's underbelly in a way that sent him galloping for the woods.

"Elayne!" Christy screamed in terror.

Ducking beneath a snow-covered pine bow, Elayne vanished into the foliage. Christy stared at the pine branches where her sister had been, then she staggered toward a fallen tree trunk, her heart beating fast with fear.

"Deep breath," she whispered, telling herself not to panic as she seated herself on the log. Panicking would be the worst thing to do.

But she didn't have any matches with which to build a fire. And she didn't know the first thing about hunting. Or which berries were good to eat and which were poisonous. The snow was getting deeper, too. Already, it was almost to the tops of her boots. Hunching her shoulders, she shivered. When she craned her head up, the trees looked so tall. Like big mean giants.

And then she heard rustling behind her!

Yelping, she whirled, her eyes darting around, searching the shadowy woods. She didn't see anything, but there were bears in there. Maybe mountain lions. As soon as it got dark, she'd see their yellow eyes looking at her.

Suddenly the wind died.

No tree branches rustled, no birds called out. The waning sun suddenly slipped behind clouds, lengthening the afternoon shadows. How could Elayne leave? Christy squeezed her eyes shut, but tears leaked out, anyway, rolling down her chapped cheeks, feeling as hot as fire. She should never have followed Elayne.

"Here."

Blinking open her eyes, swiping away tears with her one glove, Christy found herself staring at King's legs. Throwing her head back, she saw Elayne, too. "You came back!" Christy cried, relieved. The heavy snow must have muffled the sound of King's hooves.

Christy didn't even care that Elayne sounded furious. "Like, uh, are you getting on or not?"

Not wanting to do anything that could upset Elayne further, Christy quickly leaped up from the log and grabbed Elayne's down-stretched hand.

The next thing Christy knew, she was being lifted in front of her sister onto the saddle, and they were heading into the dark woods, with King's hooves churning up snow.

RYAN HAD PULLED a kitchen chair next to Joy's and draped an arm around her shoulder, making her grateful for his comforting proximity. "I can't stand sitting," she remarked.

Despite the circumstances, Ryan's mouth quirked kindly. "Good. It's impossible. Basically we've got to do one or the other. Stand or sit."

"Maybe you should have been the editor, Ryan," Joy sighed, her eyebrows knitting with fear and worry. "Oh, you know what I mean," she stormed. "I feel so useless. Why can't we at least help look?" She hadn't really wanted a response, and now her agitated eyes left his, taking in the townspeople who had come to help search and who were passing through Jon's kitchen.

After a moment, her gaze settled on the sheriff. Steve Warwick was an imposing, take-charge kind of man, big and brawny, with bunching muscles that strained his tan uniform. He had a habit of pacing—he was doing so now—as if he were a caged beast, but he also had kind brown eyes that inspired confidence that he'd find the girls. Hooking a thumb through a belt loop and letting his fingers trail on his gun holster, Steve said, "We need you two here."

Ryan nodded curtly, even though his voice said he wished it were different. "He's right, Joy. We don't know our way around the mountains. It wouldn't help for us to get lost."

Joy nodded, but she knew Ryan was only staying here to protect her in case the men found...

In case the men found...

In case...

A soft muffled cry escaped her throat.

"The girls are fine, Joy." At the gentle urgency of Ryan's words, she managed another nod, but she knew he couldn't relax any more than she could. His hand slid up her arm, then his palm cupped her shoulder and squeezed, imparting such strength that she wondered how she'd gotten through these eight months without him. Of course, she quickly reminded herself, he'd never been this supportive during the last years of their marriage. Leaning closer, so only she could hear, he whispered, "I'm scared, too, Joy."

"You are?" Her eyes darting to his, she couldn't believe that the Ryan Holt she'd married was admitting to such a thing. Or that he was reacting to the situation by comforting her instead of masking his fear with anger.

"Yeah," he repeated softly, "of course, I'm scared. And worried. But I know the kids are fine. I've got a feeling about it."

She couldn't help but offer a fleeting smile. "The new Ryan Holt relies on intuition, too?"

His dark eyes were solemn, touched by emotion, as if he were also thinking about their relationship. "He sure does."

"But the snow…" Joy's levity returned as she gazed through the window. Earlier, the beautiful, sloping, snow-covered hills had looked like a fairyland, but now, the fast-approaching twilight made the sky as gray as the kitchen countertops, and Joy's worries were painting the landscape even more darkly. Where the trees had been havens for the birds earlier, they were now thick foliage that would make it harder to find the children. Snow that had glistened in the sun was now deep enough to bury a child. And so dangerously cold. Joy's heart thudded dully. Where were her babies? Her two precious little girls? *If I'd just handled things with Elayne better, they wouldn't have run away.*

"It's still light out, Joy," Ryan assured her. Just hearing his calm, low voice helped. Still squeezing her shoulder with one hand, he slid the other under the table and found the fist she'd clenched on her thigh. Gently prying it open, he threaded his fingers through hers and pulled their joined hands onto his thigh. The heavy denim of his jeans brushed her knuckles, and she could feel subtle movements— the shift of his weight, how his muscles flexed. Settling back, she molded a shoulder into the hollow of his. With so much terror coarsing through her, she wished Ryan was even closer.

"That snow's really coming down," she murmured.

"We're doing everything possible to find your girls," Steve said, his gaze assessing Ryan's, man-to-man. "We just got the okay to borrow a county-owned helicopter from the next town over."

"A helicopter?" Joy repeated hopefully.

"Yes, ma'am. If the kids are in an area where the trees are bare, it should be easy to spot them."

Her eyes flitted to the hills again. "But there are so many evergreens."

Sheriff Warwick nodded. "Yes, ma'am. But we've got plenty of people on the ground, too."

Joy managed another nod, fighting tears as she glanced around. Practically the whole town had come. Apparently one phone call had prompted another, and even though it was Christmas, people arrived in droves, wearing heavy parkas and boots and offering pies, cakes and cookies. Nikki and Joy had laid out leftover turkey and made a pot of coffee.

"Don't you go worryin', Mrs. Holt," one big burly man said now, catching her gaze as he trooped toward the back door. "My kids have done run off in these hills more times than I can count. Bad weather never stopped 'em, neither. Believe me, we'll find your youngin's."

Joy swallowed hard. "Elayne's been taking riding lessons, and she knows a lot about horses."

Sheriff Warwick nodded. "Now you're thinking."

"But she doesn't know these mountains," Joy couldn't help adding, fear getting the best of her again.

"Maybe not *these*," Ryan soothed. "But she knows mountains."

That much was true. Joy thought of the West Virginia hills where she and Elayne had grown up. They looked much like this, thick and lush with pines. Years ago, Joy had often gone four-wheeling. Countless times, whatever adult was driving would get them lost, only to come out of the woods not ten feet from a pay phone.

Ryan's voice was a gentle rumble. "There's a few hours left until dark."

Looking out, Joy tried not to dwell on the weak winter light and thickening cloud cover.

"Jon and I know every inch of this terrain," Sheriff Warwick was assuring, both for her and Ryan's benefit. "Don't forget, we grew up here. Played cowboys and Indians. Cops and robbers. If we can't find the girls by nightfall, that means they've probably hunkered down until morning.''

Somehow, Joy managed to forced down the lump in her throat. ''But where?''

The sheriff shrugged. ''Plenty of places. Elayne's old enough to build a fire, and there're caves everywhere. Rock formations form buffers from the snow and wind, too, and there are old, unused mining shacks. Around here, you'd be hard-pressed *not* to find a place to get warm.''

Joy's fingers tightened through Ryan's. ''Christy doesn't even have her glove.''

''But a parka's gone,'' Ryan returned. ''And boots. She's dressed warmly enough, and they've got the horse.''

''Exactly.'' The sheriff leaned against the counter. ''King knows his way home. Since he hasn't come back without them yet, we know they're all still together.''

It sounded so reasonable, and Joy wanted to believe that no harm could come to the girls, but she was still worried. After a moment's silence, the wall phone rang, startling Joy. The sheriff lifted the receiver. ''Warwick here.''

It was the helicopter pilot. Joy listened intently as the sheriff specified what area the pilot should cover. Too nervous to sit another moment, she disengaged her hand from Ryan's, got up and went to the window. Standing at the sink, she clenched her hands around the edge of the counter. Outside, the shadows were lengthening. A group of men, including Jon and some of the Ryders, were gathered near a woodpile. Even with the door shut, Joy could hear the rallying male voices. Raising an arm, Jon pointed toward various sections of the woods, pairing up the men and organizing the search.

"You holdin' up okay, Joy?" Nikki bustled past with a coffeepot, patting Joy's arm.

"Isn't there anything else I can do, Nikki?" Joy felt as if she'd go crazy unless some activity took her mind from her worries.

"No, hon. You and Ryan take it easy." Nikki's voice raised. "Junior? C'mere. I need you to take this thermos out."

Just as Junior brushed past, slamming the door behind him, Ryan came up behind Joy. Once more, she was relieved by his physical presense—by the warmth of his chest against her back, and his strong, soothing hands on her shoulders.

"A lot of people are looking," he said.

Lifting a hand, she rested it on the back of his, which cupped her shoulder. "I know you're going every bit as crazy as I am, Ryan." He'd always been a man of action, the one to give orders, but now he was forced to let other men call all the shots.

As if reading her mind, he said, "It's hard to trust other people to do things right, especially when it involves something as important as the safety of our girls."

Our girls.

Her throat tightened. Ryan had always been an

uncle to Elayne, but now he'd stepped in by offering support, both financial and emotional. Since they weren't even married now, what exactly did the show of support mean? After Joy had botched the scene in the dining room so badly, it was Ryan who had followed Elayne, making sure she was okay.

"If they wind up near a phone and call," Ryan suddenly continued, "we'll be here waiting, Joy."

And if they don't…

As another whimper escaped her, Joy felt Ryan's lips brush her ear. "I told you I've got a good feeling," he assured. "C'mon, you know I've got good instincts."

The years of marriage to him told her that much. She turned toward him, and because he didn't back away, she found herself pressed against him. "Ryan?"

His eyes were unbelievably attentive. "Yeah?"

"Can we go to the barn, at least? Maybe…" Maybe the sheriff missed some clue. Oh, Joy didn't expect a note, or footprints that led into the hills, but there might be…something.

"Sure, baby," Ryan murmured, then caught the sheriff's eyes. "Mind if we go out to the barn?"

Clearly Steve Warwick would prefer they stay inside and have another cup of coffee so he wouldn't worry about losing them, too, but he seemed to understand their need to occupy themselves. "Sure," he said. "I'm heading out to meet the pilot, but Nikki'll man the phone. Right, Nikki?''

''You got it.''

Just the promise of action flooded Joy with relief. Quickly she and Ryan headed for the hallway. Finding her coat in a closet, she shrugged into it.

''Baby,'' Ryan murmured again. Under other circumstances, the soft huskiness of his voice would have bespoken seduction. ''Wait a minute.''

Joy's eyes raised to his. ''What?''

''Here.'' Leaning, he slowly buttoned the coat she'd carelessly left open in the rush to get outside. When the top was secured under her chin, he stretched his hands around her waist, found her belt and tied it, then burrowed in her pockets for gloves. ''Your catching pneumonia won't help, either,'' he said with a chiding smile that made her throat close, aching with emotion. It was so long since Ryan had been this concerned about her. But once upon a time, he'd always been this sweet. This kind. This loving.

Loving.

Yes, that was definitely the word. Right now, they were loving each other. Treating each other with all the kindness, tenderness and respect they'd lost. Her eyes stung with unshed tears as she reached for the bottom of his shearling jacket, then zipped it all the way up to his chin. ''Wouldn't want you to catch cold, either,'' she said shakily.

With the slight lift of his lips, amber light came

into his eyes. "How've I been dressing myself all these months?"

She couldn't answer because the swift tug of her heart stole her breath. Their mouths were just inches apart, and Ryan tilted his head and surveyed her—so long that she knew he saw the vulnerability in her eyes. When his lips parted, she was sure he was going to kiss her, too, but he merely slid a hand beneath her elbow and guided her toward the back door.

The cold was bracing. Joy drew a deep gasp of it as Ryan caught her hand, snuggled it into his pocket, then headed for the barn, waving at the men by the woodpile. So close to Ryan, feeling his warmth, Joy let her eyes trail from the barn to the gray shadows it cast over the snow. Cold flakes touched her face as her eyes searched the hillside, and as Ryan pulled open the barn's heavy door, she was silently praying for the return of the girls. It was warmer inside, sheltered from the wind. Slowly they walked the length of the barn, their hips brushing as they passed stalls and a tack room, their eyes scanning the floor, looking for something.

"See anything?" Ryan asked.

She shook her head as they reached the opposite door.

"Maybe out here," Ryan said, opening it.

The area just beyond the door was partially shielded from the wind by an awning, and prints were in the snowdrift. "Hooves," Joy said, pointing, her eyes welling with tears. "And Elayne's and

Christy's boots.'' As she stared down, a swift gust
of wind came, blowing powder across the prints,
making them fade before her eyes. Soon, the prints,
like the children, would be gone.

Ryan stepped closer in the shadowy enclave.
''Shh…''

Now that they were away from the brightly lit
kitchen and the eyes of so many strangers, her voice
caught with panic. ''I can't imagine them out here
alone, Ryan!''

She wasn't prepared for him to disentangle their
twined fingers. Or for the fierce way he wrapped
his arms around her, suddenly crushing her to his
chest. His voice was low, muffled by a howl of
wind. ''Whatever happens,'' he whispered against
her cheek, ''I'm here. I'm with you, Joy.''

Gazing up at him in the snowy twilight, she
could see their fogged breath mixing. Hugging his
waist, she said, ''You've changed so much, Ryan.''

Despite the circumstances, a smile touched his
lips, though worry over the children didn't allow it
to reach his eyes. ''God knows I've tried.''

Her voice was a whisper, barely audible in the
wind. ''I'm glad.''

''Do you like me better now?'' he whispered
back.

''I think so.''

She'd loved him—married him—the way he was.
But how had she managed to lose him just as he
became the kind of man she could rely on? Suddenly, she'd admitted how much she wanted him

back. She couldn't go on living without him. Quickly she ducked her chin, to hide the power of the revelation, but her helpless eyes shot to his again. Did he want her anymore? Maybe a little?

He pulled her closer, saying words she so much needed to hear. "You're a great mother. You couldn't have done any better than you did. Elayne's coming here today was a shock. Remember when you wanted to quit work and stay home with Christy?"

She relaxed against his chest, the soft suede finish of his coat brushing her cheek when she nodded.

"It was me who wanted you to keep working. I…liked being married to the woman who could do it all. I was proud. I know I pushed you to—"

She shook her head. "We needed the money. It's not your fault."

"We could have done without."

"Anyway—" Her eyes darted to his. "It doesn't matter anymore."

"Matters to me." His eyes turned darker in the dim light, and his voice became fierce. "It matters because you've always been willing to take responsibility for everything. And now, I won't let you blame yourself for what the kids have done. They're old enough to know better than to run off like this."

Tears threatened again, stinging in Joy's eyes like the wind, and her quickened breath pulled in Ryan's sharp male smell. Sensing her emotion, he squeezed his biceps tighter around her, so tight that his arms felt like bands of pure strength.

She tilted up her face to find him looking right into her eyes. Nestling closer, he let their noses touch before his mouth dropped a fraction, settling open-lipped onto hers. A soft moan rose from her throat as his parted lips moved, molding around her lower one, offering the exact kiss she needed. A kiss that was quiet in the wind, warm in the cold…a kiss that soothed worry and made promises against loneliness.

When her lower lip was thoroughly dampened, he gently captured her tongue and deepened the kiss until she was opening her mouth all the way for him. It was an intimacy they'd shared thousands of times, but this seemed so different…so new. Each slow, thrusting stroke of Ryan's tongue was a reminder of all that had once bound them, and yet like nothing she'd ever felt. She melted against him.

After a moment, he quit kissing and merely held her. Leaning away a fraction, she stared toward the children's footprints just as another windy gust stirred the snow. Fine grains of powdery white dust were blown across the prints, then once more. A last chilly blow covered them completely.

Her voice caught. "Oh, Ryan, I'm so glad you're here."

"I know," he whispered, locking his lips on hers once more. As his arms enveloped her, the fear of loss overwhelmed her. Life was so fragile. Swaying with Ryan in the wind, Joy thought, *Don't leave me again, Ryan. You're all I have.*

Chapter Eight

All day, as the passing clouds gave way to a rose twilight and clear starry night, Ryan watched the fear in Joy's eyes deepen. Now, standing with her in the dimly lit upstairs hallway at Jon's, he gently rubbed a thumb across her wrinkled forehead, smoothing the furrows. When her trusting eyes gazed at him from under knitted blond eyebrows, Ryan's heart swelled with the desire to put things right for all of them. If only he knew where the kids were.

"I know it's hard, but try to get some sleep," he said, then unable to help himself, he leaned and quickly brushed his lips across hers.

Her voice sounded far away. "See you in the morning, Ryan."

It hurt to leave her. But if he took her in his arms as he had at the barn, it would threaten his control—hers, too—so Ryan crossed the hallway. As his hand closed over the knob of the opposite bedroom, he turned and looked at her again, but she was staring through a window. She said, "Do you really think we should stay here?"

"As opposed to?"

"Staying at the inn. What if the kids try to call us there?"

"We were here when they left. And the Scudders will answer the phone at the inn all night. The sheriff really seems to think there are plenty of places out there where the kids can get warm," he added, even if the assurances couldn't stop him and Joy from worrying. "Besides..." *Who knows where they are now?* Through the window, not much could be seen. Just shades of the dark night, moon and stars. And Joy's reflection in the glass. She looked beautiful, if emotionally wrung out. The worried fingers she'd dragged through her short blond hair had left it hopelessly mussed in a way that made Ryan think of combing it for her and, hours ago, she'd eaten the lipstick that usually kept her mouth looking as red and plump as a cherry.

And she's way over there.

Joy might as well have been on the opposite coast of the country where she was living. Still, even if they'd chosen to be apart, this moment felt strained. How could they be entering separate bedrooms when they so desperately needed to hold each other? Not twenty-four hours ago, they'd been wrapped naked in a quilt at the inn, and Ryan had been trying to convince himself that things were different now, that Joy had changed as much as he had.

Heavy treads of boots sounded from downstairs, bringing him back to the present, reminding him that people would be coming and going all night, still searching. Glancing toward the stairs, he had to fight not to go back down, but Sheriff Warwick was right. He and Joy needed sleep. Besides, if Ryan stayed downstairs, Joy would insist on being with him.

But separate bedrooms?

"Joy?"

The clear emerald eyes that had first mesmerized Ryan nine years ago widened as if Joy knew exactly what was on his mind. "What, Ryan?"

Was that hope in her voice? Need for him? Just this once, he wished she'd be the one to initiate things, to say she didn't want to be alone.

Lying across the hall by himself, worrying about the kids, he knew he'd go insane without her. Vague discomfort uncoiled in him as he thought about the kiss in the barn—and about how fast it had turned molten. Even more dangerous were the memories of how protective he'd felt toward Joy, how moved. All day, their warm embrace in the freezing snow had stayed with him. Abruptly he released the doorknob. Biting back an oath at his own lack of resolve, he strode across the hallway again, stopping in front of her.

Her voice skipped with uncertainty. "Ryan?"

His voice, already lowered with worry, dropped an octave with her nearness. "I want to hold you again." Relieved when she didn't protest, he glided his hands around the gentle curve of her waist, pulling her close while he let his whole body sink down against hers. As she leaned back against the door frame, their hips locked and chests and bellies brushed. Hours ago, she'd removed her jacket, and now his breath quickened when he felt her skin pulse beneath a soft black sweater. Lingering traces of her perfume made his nostrils flare, then he realized it wasn't the perfume, but the absence of it— the womanly scent that perfume no longer hid. Joy had worn off the perfume hours ago.

It was wrong, but he leaned away saying, "I know we're divorced, but can we go to bed together? The way we're supposed to?"

"*Supposed* to?"

Yeah. Because we're made for each other. At least when we're in bed. "I need you to…" Ryan's voice trailed off, his eyes skimming the delicate pale skin of her jaw, then dropping to the gentle curve of her neck. He could see the rapid beat of her pulse.

She'd raised an eyebrow. "Need me to…?"

Even sessions with Laura hadn't enabled Ryan to handle the sudden rush of vulnerability that turned his tone coarser and made his words uncharacteristically tentative. "To do what you… well, what you do for me, Joy." He didn't mean to be vague, but did he really have to explain?

Her eyes widened. "You're saying you want sex right now Ryan?"

"No!" Quickly he shook his head. He only

wanted to be with her. For once, maybe he needed her strength. He'd never known she possessed so much. All day, she'd kept a level head and he'd felt oddly proud. Blowing out a frustrated sigh, he lifted a hand from her waist and raked it through his hair. "Maybe I *am* thinking about sex," he admitted. "I don't really know. I'm confused." It was hard to admit. Maybe he'd never even said those words to her before. "But when bad things happen," he continued, "you've always known how to take my mind away. And right now, with the kids gone..." He glanced around again, hearing the tread of boots and feeling unaccustomed helplessness.

"You want to go away, Ryan?"

"Only with you. Or to wherever the kids are." Thinking of them again, his emotions threatened to overwhelm him. His penetrating eyes sought hers— and he dared to imagine that she, too, needed a soothing touch only he could offer. Reaching for her, he grazed a thumb beneath her lower lip. Couldn't they share some warmth against the cold? A moment's peace from their fears about the children's safety? They'd been together last night, after all. What would be the harm?

"You're really worried, aren't you, Ryan?"

"Of course I am." How could she even ask? But he knew why she had. In situations such as this, he usually used anger to push away his real feelings, and she sensed that the changes in him made living with doubt more difficult. "I can't turn off my emotions the way I used to,'' he said. Not after spilling his guts to Laura.

"Emotions are meant to be shared."

"You didn't share yours about Elayne." *All those years you kept me in the dark.* He was barely able to believe it still.

"I was scared."

If that was her out, he could take it, too. "So was I, Joy."

Her eyes narrowed curiously. "Of what?"

He took a deep breath, then said, "Of not being a big enough man for you." He'd barely been more than a kid when they married. He was still a student and had never even had a job, except in his dad's hardware store, so he'd desperately needed to be king of the roost—Joy's protector, her provider. He'd become those things. But looking at her now, he knew they'd have been better off if he'd simply learned to make himself more emotionally available.

A slight flush was rising in her cheeks. "You're enough of a man, Ryan."

The admission tugged at what was most masculine in him, turning his voice throatier. "Even now?"

She nodded slowly. "Especially now."

If the kids weren't gone, maybe he could have smiled. "Sure you don't miss me playing the strong man?"

The near-flicker of humor passing her lips didn't

touch the dark shadows in her eyes. "Being able to share your emotions *is* a strength."

She was right, of course. He nodded again, and as he looked at her crystal green eyes and small pert mouth, his heart seemed to turn over. Everything about her made him ache from his chest to his groin. Especially when her eyes darted to the bedroom door, reminding him she'd once been his.

All his to do with as he wanted.

How many times had he unapologetically wrapped possessive arms around her? Or slowly undressed her? Or laid her across beds and enjoyed how she watched him strip? They'd done so much—and all without understanding how fragile love was, how easily it could be lost.

And how hard you sometimes had to work to keep it.

"Ryan, what are you thinking?"

An uncharacteristic flush crept up his neck.

"What?" Joy urged.

He shrugged again, his worry for the children still in mind as he spoke. "I was thinking about right after we met, when we went away to Rhode Island for the weekend. We'd just made love at the motel, and you were hiding under the covers."

"I didn't hide."

"Did, too. But I pulled you from bed, and led you into the shower." Pausing, he pictured her as she'd been then—nine years younger, with hair long enough to brush against her breasts.

"And?"

He shook his head, thinking he'd been every bit as nervous as she. "When we were both under the water, you started touching me." Ryan's voice lowered another notch, as he remembered the painfully calculated movements of the hand she'd glided across his soaped belly and onto his thigh. The sudden thudding of his heart stole his breath as he said, "You were so shy, baby."

Her voice caught. "Why would you remember that now?"

He shrugged again. Maybe because her touch had maddened him more than anything he'd imagined a female could do to him. Or because he'd already known he was going to marry her. His gaze softened. "Because we were so in love, Joy."

"We were," she whispered.

So, stay with me tonight. If only for old times and the way things used to be. He didn't have to ask again. Without another word, Joy stepped back, opening the door in invitation. Silently he followed her inside the bedroom.

Either Jon or Nikki had built a fire in the fireplace, and seeing that it blazed brightly, Ryan didn't bother to turn on the light. Or close the curtains. Even though he knew the girls wouldn't actually signal through the window, he couldn't shut out the night. Not when they were out there.

Joy turned to him in the firelight.

His eyes caught hers, flickering down where the flames played on her skin in shadows. He couldn't believe the rawness or depth of emotion in his own voice. "Baby," he whispered. "Please come to me."

She hesitated just a moment, pausing by the window as if intending to stand vigil.

He whispered, "You've got to rest."

Gazing back into his eyes, Joy gave a solemn little nod.

He watched her—just as he'd wanted to—savoring her walk to the bed, how the high-heeled boots she wore made her hips sway while the legs of her black slacks rustled in the silence. Drawing an inadvertent sharp breath, he watched as she slid onto the bed, slipping off the boots before pulling her feet onto the top of the spread. Seating himself on the other side, he kicked off his boots, then stripped off his undershirt and sweater and scooted toward her. He pulled her against his bare chest.

"Worried sigh," she whispered.

"Worried sigh," he whispered back—feeling her lips on his shoulder. Slender fingers trailed up his ribs, grazing his nipples and instantly making them hard.

"I...I wanted you to come in here with me," she confessed, now using his chest for a pillow and wrapping her arms around his neck. "I'm too worried and scared to be alone."

He nodded, wishing as he so often had that she could have said so sooner. All she had to do was voice her needs—and he'd be there for her, to give her what she wanted. Sighing, he sank his head into a pillow stuffed with down. "It's okay to need me,

Joy.'' At least right now. About tomorrow, Ryan wasn't so sure.

"Ryan." She sighed again. "What if…"

Tightening his arms around her back, he shushed her with a gentle kiss, then smoothed a palm over her hair. As it brushed his hand, his heart swelled almost painfully with the need to offer more than this simple comfort. "They're fine. Try to sleep," he whispered.

"I can't."

"You can."

After a long moment, she glanced up, and he ducked, his lips sinking onto hers, locking tightly over them, because he needed to share things for which he didn't have words. Shifting his weight, he pulled her on top of him, moaning as he felt the gentle pressure of her body, the insistent bones of her pelvis pushing against the already thickening swell of his desire. From under the soft wool of her sweater, her nipples tightened, making him imagine what was to come, how the wetness of his mouth might close over the straining peaks.

Releasing another moan, he thrust his tongue deeper between her lips, kissing her until her arching back brought her hips harder to him. Breathlessly leaning away, he registered both the sensual need and worry darkening her eyes, and he realized he was prepared to do anything to make her forget the fears they shared. His own head hurt from tension, his muscles were sore from all the worry.

He quickly removed her sweater, and as it came

over her head, he splayed a hand on her bottom, pressing her close and making her aware of the erection under the stiff denim he wore. Not even another kiss could cure the dryness of his mouth now, but his tongue skimmed his lips as his eyes took in her bra. It offered no support—her firm breasts didn't need it—and her constricted nipples were reddened and visible, pushing against the peekaboo cups.

Under normal circumstances, seeing Joy's body made him lose control of himself. But now, with his heightened need to escape tension and worry, Ryan fell to her—flicking open the bra's front clasp, palming the mounds, caressing their undersides. He moved between them with his mouth, feeding on the love-hardened tips until her whimpers had him suckling with fast-building hunger. Groaning, he pulled down her slacks and panties, then his hand glided down to the part of her thighs—seeking and finding her silken-haired curve.

"No," she whimpered, her legs pressing virginally together at the first shock of touch, then opening again, now completely. "No. No, Ryan."

Years of knowing—and loving—her told him she meant yes right now, so he simply settled his mouth over hers again, stifling sobs with wet kisses. Practiced fingers spread intimate moist folds so he could stroke the hard-nubbed source of her pleasure, and then he slid in a finger, moving it until she was burying soft tufts of breath on his shoulder. He could feel her readiness, her heat, but somehow—just once—he wished she'd voice her need aloud right now.

I need you, Ryan.

"Oh, Joy," he gasped, deep-kissing her, speaking her name so thickly that the word barely got out. Leaving her open legs quivering, he hurried with his jeans—pushing them down, kicking them off. Then, with his eyes blazing desire, and his soul crying out with the knowledge that he might never comfort her like this again after tonight, he began caressing her once more in a tender way that made his own loins ache.

"I miss you," he said thickly.

"I miss you, too."

He didn't know where the words came from—they just came, as did the sudden fierce plea of his voice. "What are we going to do? I can't live without you, Joy. I'm telling you, I can't." His arousal announced the truth of it, but before she could answer, Ryan's mouth settled on hers again—kissing hard, in a way that demanded every bit of her tongue, and he thrust fingers into her hair, while her hand found his shoulders and clung, her short, bitten nails digging into his skin, driving him mad. *I love her,* he thought, his heart stuttering, beating erratically. Shifting his weight, he elicited a sharp cry from her as he let his unsheathed male heat touch where she was ready.

She was as small as he remembered—small in a way that threatened his control, and small in a way he hadn't fully enjoyed last night in his rush to possess her. He meant to enjoy it now. Speaking in a strangled voice as he started entering her, he said, "Joy, no man feels this for a woman he can live without. No man feels…" *So much love, baby. Or so much heartbreak.*

As her sweet, damp folds opened and closed around him, she shuddered beneath him. "No. No man feels this, Joy," he assured her with a sudden growl as he thrust deep, then began loving her, ever so slowly, so they could gasp and murmur together, with her saying, "I know the kids are all right. I believe your intuition. But they're a handful. I can't raise them by myself."

Him saying, "I know. I can help. I miss you so much. I dream about you every night, and wake up hard and wanting."

Moments later, with his eyes as hungry as fire seeking oxygen, he raggedly said, "I love you, Joy. When we're making love like this…" Her enveloping heat took the whole length of him and his breath. When he could speak again, he croaked, "You love me?"

"You know it," she cried.

In the back of his mind were warnings about speaking in the heat of passion. Warnings, since their problems hadn't changed. But as his mouth drank from hers, and she arched to take him with so much greed, he no longer cared. With his mind hazier, his climax nearing, he gasped, "Marry me again—"

On a sharp intake of breath, she cried, "You're coming home?"

The words were wrenched from his throat. "I can't even tie my ties—"

"Only you can fix that stupid door."

Another strangled cry came, this one from low in Ryan's belly. He couldn't hold on another second—no more than he could take his release without her. His voice was strained to breaking. "Come on, Joy." And then she was blessedly his. Her climax freed him—and his wild release flowed, the warmth filling her. *Without protection.*

"What are we going to do?" she whispered when her breath quieted. "Oh, Ryan…"

He silenced her with a kiss. His voice was still dry and hoarse from all the strangled words he'd uttered. "First," he whispered huskily, "we have to find our kids. And then…"

Her silken hair teased the sensitized tip of a nipple as she raised her head to gaze into his eyes. "Then?"

His eyes held hers. "Then we have to get remarried, Joy."

She didn't look nearly as certain, so he didn't pursue it, but scooted back the covers, urging her beneath, and pressing her cheek to his chest. "Just shut your eyes," he whispered. "Go to sleep."

Not that he could. His gaze drifted to the window, as his soothing palm slid up and down Joy's naked back. Where on earth were the girls?

CHRISTY REWRAPPED Elayne's scarf around her ungloved hand, then took a steadying hold on the pommel, so she could wrench around in the saddle. Even in the dark, she could tell Elayne was freezing. She was hunkered over and shivering, her arms bracketing Christy's sides, her hands gripping the reins. Her skin looked bloodlessly pale in the moonlight, her lips blue. Staring forward again, Christy took in the dark bobbing silhouette of King's massive head. "I'm cold," she groaned, her teeth chattering. "Should we have stayed in that cave?"

"I don't know," Elayne murmured.

Christy tried to tell herself it wasn't so bad. Body heat helped. With the horse beneath her and Elayne behind her, she was at least shielded from the wind. Still, she couldn't help but add, "And I'm scared, Elayne."

Elayne's breath warmed Christy's cheek. "I know you are."

Christy shuddered, her gaze sweeping over the stars that glittered in the clear dark sky. "We're still lost aren't we?" she continued in a small voice.

Elayne didn't say anything, which Christy decided meant yes.

Animal sounds filled the night—hoots and growls, and stealthy rustlings in the trees that made Christy long for the protection of the cave. Elayne had even built a fire in the enclosure, but then they'd run out of dry sticks and matches.

"Forget about it," Elayne had said as the last ember burned out. "We'll just have to go back."

Angrily she'd toed the ground. "Not that I'm ever living with Aunt...with Joy."

Christy hadn't said anything. But Aunt May was dead, so Christy didn't really think Elayne had a choice. "Are you going to try to get adopted?" she'd asked.

"I don't know," Elayne had replied, shooting her a mean look that meant the conversation was over.

Now Elayne lifted the reins and pointed. "Christy?" she said in a worried tone that wasn't any more comforting than the darkness and howling wind. "Remember those boulders?"

Christy stared at the rocks. "I dunno. Maybe." Everything looked the same. They'd been riding for hours—following various paths, going in circles. Once, they'd gone down the mountain, figuring they'd eventually find a road. They never did.

Christy's eyes pierced the darkness. For a long time, she saw only snow. And then a light suddenly flickered through the trees. She pointed excitedly. "Look!"

"Good going, Christy. It's something. Even if it's way down the mountain."

Despite the circumstances, Christy brimmed with pride. And then she ventured, "If you go and get adopted, Elayne, could you still be my sister?"

Barely perceptibly, Elayne's arms tightened where they bracketed Christy's waist. "We *are* sisters, Christy."

Christy's heart skipped a beat. "Good," she whispered. And taking in the light in the distance, she silently added, *deep sigh of relief.*

Chapter Nine

In Christy's dream, some old man was talking to himself, saying, "What've you gone and done now, Hubert? Why, Pam ought never have married the likes of you. You're dang lucky she hasn't tanned your sorry hide. What if you really *had* sold this here place to a big city shyster? No sir, no matter how bad you's a wantin' to retire, you can't sell off your history. 'Course if that big city feller ain't lyin' about his plans, then things'll work out pretty good, I guess..."

When all that followed was unintelligible mumbling, Christy drifted deeper into sleep, curling her knees up and snuggling. After a moment, the funny old man in her dream, muttered, "Folks useta travel far and wide, lookin' for spots in these here mountains where they could settle down and raise youngin's. Now what would a city feller know about that? Or about diggin' up arrowheads 'round these parts? He wouldn't know there's an Indian burial mound up on Sky Bluff, neither. Or that kids go

campin' there, tell ghost stories and scare the be-
jesus out of themselves.

"Well, maybe that feller's boss and wife was
right. Maybe he's gonna turn the inn into one of
them strip malls. Aw, Huburt, you're a dumb cuss.
What makes you think he wasn't lyin' about his
plans?"

Sighing, Christy wished the man would get out
of her dreams since he was waking her up. Determined to ignore him, she wiggled down, working
her mouth so that whatever was tickling her lower
lip would quit. Just as she realized it was a piece
of hay, the old man started talking again.

"Well...you gotta feel sorry for him, even if he
does build them strip malls. Hang-fire, with his kids
done runaway and all, I figure the feller's got
enough on his mind, without worrying over some
fool inn."

When the voice dropped again, Christy uttered a
peeved grunt. Why did *he* have to be in her dream?
Why couldn't she get some nice lady who sang lul-
labies? Or somebody who was cooking breakfast—
since her tummy was rumbling?

"Can't let the old place go to pot, though," the
old man continued. "No, sir. 'Specially not after all
me 'n Pam done accomplished here—gettin'
hitched and raisin' up three youngin's. But we can't
keep the inn up no more, not without some help.
What, with her arthritis and all, Pam can't garden.
And I sure ain't what I used to be." He heaved a

loud sigh. "Pam sure did used to love them flowers, though."

Christy tried burrowing her ear to muffle the sound. Suddenly she realized that the warmth beside her wasn't a blanket. It was Elayne. Briefly slitting open an eye, Christy glimpsed her sister's navy pea coat. Hmm. No wonder her cheek itched; it was pressed against scratchy wool.... As Christy yawned, the closing corners of her mouth curled into a smile. Her big sister's arm was draped across her back, keeping her warm.

We're sisters.

Last night, Christy was starting to panic when she saw the light flickering in the distance. "Don't worry," Elayne had said, urging King on. "Like, maybe that's a house or something. Maybe they'll let us stay the night."

But distance was deceiving. At least another mile of dark shadows and snow-covered hills lay between them and the light. Shivering, they'd finally reached a carriage house. It was seemingly unused, but the electricity was on and there was an overhead light. Elayne had found a space heater in a musty storeroom. Together, she and Christy ripped hay from a bale, spread it on the floor and then covered it with a musty-smelling plaid horse blanket.

"Here," Elayne had said, once they were settled, pulling out some food she'd been hoarding—a hunk of bread and slices of turkey—which they'd eaten with relish. "Tomorrow, when it's light, we can figure out where we are."

When they heard a helicopter—and not for the first time—their eyes met, but Elayne wasn't ready to be found yet. She'd tilted her head, listening, and announced, "I'm not going to New York."

What Elayne meant was that she wasn't going to live with their mother. Christy had remained silent, but she'd wanted to assure Elayne that New York was nice, with a comfortable apartment and lots of things to do. Maybe Elayne could even share Christy's bedroom, which was decorated with peach walls and a butter yellow bedspread. Finally she'd ventured, "New York is okay."

Elayne had shrugged. "It could be really cool. I don't care."

"I don't blame you, I guess," Christy had admitted. Why hadn't their mom talked to Elayne after the fight in the dining room? And why hadn't she told Elayne the truth sooner? Knowing she'd miss her bedroom, Christy'd said, "Well, I guess I won't go home, either. I'll stay with you."

Elayne had looked at her a long time. Despite the warmth of the space heater, Elayne's breath still fogged the air. "You'd do that? Go wherever I go?"

Christy had nodded solemnly, edging closer and slipping a hand into Elayne's. An awkward second passed, then Elayne's hand closed around hers and squeezed.

Elayne had suddenly sighed. "Oh, forget it. I mean, where could we go, anyway?"

"My daddy's," Christy had offered.

Elayne was suddenly blinking back tears. "Uncle Ryan did say it would be okay. Maybe we'll go there, Christy."

For a long time, they'd sat silently. When they snuggled down on the horse blanket, Christy had edged closer, and after a tentative moment, Elayne's arm draped across her back.

"Elayne?" Christy had whispered.

"Hmm?"

"Are you going to be my sister only right now? Or could you be my sister later, too?" *Maybe for keeps?*

During the ensuing silence, Christy listened to all the strange sounds—the carriage house door banging on its hinges, the howling wind, Elayne's slow, steady breath. "Don't worry about it, anymore," Elayne finally said. "We'll be sisters from now on."

"I wasn't worried," Christy declared, even though she had been. And then, after a moment, she added the word, "sis."

Elayne made a sound between a sigh and chuckle. "'Night, sis," she'd returned.

Suddenly Christy's eyes flew open as the annoying man in her dream intruded on the pleasant memories.

"Dang!" he burst out.

He was no dream man. It was Hub Scudder. He hadn't seen her and Elayne yet, but he was coming toward them, dragging a hand distractedly through his bushy gray hair while he thoughtfully tongued his chipped front tooth. "I know I didn't leave that space heater on. Didn't even know the thing was still out here. And I didn't leave on no light, even if Pam done sworn I did."

Suddenly he saw them. Stopping in his tracks, he hooked a thumb through the suspender beneath his open jeans jacket and said, "Well, I'll be."

"Mr. Scudder?" Keeping her eyes on Hub and shaking her sister's shoulder, Christy lowered her voice. "Elayne. Wake up, Elayne!"

Finally Elayne blinked sleepily.

"Your folks is fit to be hog-tied," Hub announced sternly. "Now you youngin's git yourselves up right now, and into the house. You must be hungry and Pam's done made some ham and biscuits this mornin'."

"Yes, sir," Christy said contritely. But as Elayne scooted up beside her, Christy giggled, since hay was sticking up every which way in Elayne's hair.

Hub shook his head. "Dang if you two didn't look like angels, all curled up together. Lyin' in a manger as sure as the baby Jesus on Christmas morning. 'Course Christmas was yesterday. And today you two's run off like the spawn of the devil. Now git, ya hear? We'd better phone your folks and tell 'em you's all right."

"Sorry, Mr. Scudder." Christy groggily stumbled to her feet, nearly tripping over her rubber boots.

He put his hands on his hips. "You and your

sister are a handful, aren't you?'' he asked rhetorically.

You and your sister.

Feeling proprietary, Christy grabbed Elayne's hand and followed Hub toward the inn. *Your sister.* Christy definitely liked the sound of that. It was funny, she thought, that overnight she'd found a big sister who would watch over her for the rest of her life.

No matter where Elayne went, Christy was going there, too.

"THEY'VE BEEN FOUND?" *Thank God,* Joy thought, placing a trembling hand on the kitchen counter. From what she gleaned from the phone conversation, the Scudders had found the kids asleep in an old carriage house adjacent to the inn. Never taking her eyes from Ryan's, Joy pulled nervously at the hem of a gray crew-neck sweater Nikki had given her this morning, smoothing it over her slacks.

"Yes," Ryan was saying into the receiver. "We'll be right there. Hub...no, you don't need to bring them. We'll hop in the car and come get them."

"Are they all right, Ryan?" Joy murmured worriedly, not wanting to interrupt the conversation, but needing reassurance. Only now did she realize how worried she'd been; even though the kids were safe, she didn't quite believe it. And yet, she knew it was true—and felt lighter than air.

Maybe it's not all relief. Maybe it's because I'm in love again.

Still listening to Ryan, Joy acknowledged the truth of it. She'd always want the man whose penetrating dark eyes lasered into hers as he spoke on the phone. What woman wouldn't? Ryan had always exuded sex and strength. But now he'd harnessed that strength, controlling it. Right now, the power of it emanated from his body even though he wasn't moving, but only leaning against the counter with the phone tucked under his chin. Joy's eyes trailed up the muscles that were subtly visible through yesterday's jeans, to the cardigan he'd borrowed from Jon. Ryan hadn't yet shaved, and the hint of whiskers and his finger-combed hair gave him a careless look.

No, no man could be more physically appealing to her. And last night...

As he continued asking questions about the girls, a lump formed in Joy's throat. Last night, they'd become man and wife again. He'd asked her to marry him, and she'd accepted. Somehow, they'd agreed, they'd work out the problems that had destroyed their marriage.

Now Ryan's mouth was compressing grimly, though his dark intelligent eyes were still on Joy's. "Thanks, Hub. Would you mind putting the girls on the line? I think their mother would like to speak to them."

Her heart skipped a beat. Yes, she definitely

wanted to hear their voices. She'd tried to be positive last night, but she wouldn't have made it without Ryan. Way back in her mind, Joy had feared she'd never see Christy again, that there'd be no opportunity to set things right with Elayne.

Suddenly Ryan's gaze shifted away. His voice toughened, his anger rising. "Please," he said. "Put them on anyway."

Joy edged closer, her eyes flitting between the receiver and Ryan. "They don't want to talk to us?"

Ryan didn't affirm or deny, just began chewing his lower lip in agitation. "I don't care what you want, Elayne," he said into the phone now. "The least you can do is apologize to your mother, and let her know—" Apparently Elayne cut him off. A few seconds later, Ryan spoke again, his voice cold. "You've no idea how worried we were. Don't you even care what you put us through?"

Reaching out, Joy laid a staying hand on his arm. "Please," she implored.

He sighed, covering the receiver. "Please *what?*"

"Please don't yell at her, Ryan."

Releasing a frustrated breath, he looked at Joy as if she was crazy. "You don't think I should yell?"

No. Please. Don't do anything to alienate her from us. With a gentleness she hoped would diffuse his temper, she said, "You've been doing such a good job of keeping your anger under control." Lowering her voice further, she coaxed, "We can't afford to scare Elayne away. She's…so lost right now. She has every right to be angry with me.''

"Every right?" Ryan's hand was clamped so hard over the mouthpiece that his knuckles were turning white. "Why?"

Because I gave her away. Joy stared at Ryan, unable to say the words.

"And you're going to let her blackmail you with the guilt? For how long, Joy?" Fury suddenly danced in his dark eyes, bringing them to life and making them glitter. "Joy," he continued, "you did what you thought was right. And if you had it to do over again tomorrow, you might well do the exact same thing.''

Maybe. But Joy's own children had run away because of her, and now they didn't even want to speak to her.

Uncovering the mouthpiece, Ryan said, "Your mother and I are on our way." After another pause, he continued, "Sorry, Elayne. But your *mother* is coming.''

Joy's heart was pounding wildly as Ryan hung up the phone. "She's not ready to call me mother. She might never be. So, why did you keep calling me that, Ryan?''

Ryan shook his head in thorough exasperation. "Because you *are* her mother, Joy.''

How could Ryan be so dense? "But for so long, she thought May was…''

His glittering eyes turned a shade darker. "May's dead.''

"Don't be mean."

"I'm not being mean. I'm being a realist."

From inches away, his challenging flinty gaze bore into her. It had been so long since she'd seen Ryan mad like this that Joy had forgotten the electric heat that emanated from his skin. She could almost feel the fury pumping through his veins. Despite the tension that filled him, he reached out, and the touch to her cheek was gentle.

A second later, his hands settled more possessively on her waist, urging her closer. The perfect fit of their bodies made her ache. Last night, everything had seemed so clear. Last night, it was all going to work out. The kids would soon be home. She and Ryan would remarry.

"Don't be angry with me," she said.

His body said he wasn't but his eyes remained livid. "In the past," he said, his voice low, "I know I've used anger when I felt other things—confusion...fear...regret. But right now, I'm mad, Joy. Just plain mad. And there's nothing wrong with that. It's a valid feeling. Elayne's thirteen and she knew better than to pull a stunt like this. She took off with Christy. God knows what could have happened to them." He paused, his smoldering eyes flickering over her, this time with awareness that made her breasts tighten. His voice turned huskier, "Now, c'mon. Get your coat. We're going after them."

"I'm staying here."

"Like hell."

The pulse ticked too fast in her throat, making her breathless. "Why is it always so hard to stand up to you?" she muttered.

"You have trouble standing up to anybody."

Even though it was the truth, she balked. But on this, he had to see her point. "Don't you understand? The kids don't want me there right now." She glanced away, her heart pulling. "I'd rather die than alienate them."

When she looked into Ryan's eyes again, he was surveying her coolly, with barely masked temper that made her heart break. Could they fight—and stay together? It was so important that she know. Everything seemed so tenuous, and she couldn't live with the ambiguity.

"The kids are kids," he said simply. "So, I really don't give a damn what they want." And then, suddenly gliding a hand beneath Joy's elbow, he all but manhandled her toward the hallway.

ELAYNE'S GREEN EYES flashed. "You can't make me go to New York with *her,* Uncle Ryan!"

Barely noticing the inn's old-fashioned drawing room where they were seated, Ryan gripped the arms of an overstuffed armchair, leaned forward and glared at the girls. Between their grimy, rumpled clothes and the hay sticking from their hair, they looked worse for the wear. Seated on a sofa, they were staring back at Ryan with their arms crossed defensively. Since Elayne had pulled her hair back into a ponytail, the earring locked into her eyebrow looked even more menacing than usual. Ryan just hoped she hadn't put a tattoo on some part of herself he hadn't yet seen.

"Your mother's right outside," she said. "And when she comes in, we're all going to discuss this. I know you're hurt, Elayne—"

"I'm not *hurt!* I'd never let somebody like *her* hurt me!" The betrayal in Elayne's eyes said differently. "Besides, you swore I could stay with you, Uncle Ryan. And Christy's coming."

Deep breath. These kids were trying his patience. "I said if I'm around, you'll always have a home, but you're not going to use me to hide behind. You've got to deal with what's happened. And that means talking to your mother."

Elayne stared at him, slack-jawed. "She's the one hiding in the hallway!"

Good point. But Joy wasn't hiding out of fear. She was trying to make this easy for Elayne. Not that he had. Already, he'd come at both kids by raising holy hell. A few moments ago, he'd promised numerous modes of punishment. "You're not going to railroad your mother." *Or me.*

Elayne said nothing; she merely hugged her arms tightly to her chest and stared through a leaded casement window. Ryan glanced toward an empty doorway leading into the hallway, wondering if Joy was listening. Couldn't she see that her daughters needed her to be an angry parent? Their misbehavior could have brought serious consequences, and that had to be addressed.

The longer he stared at the doorway, though, the angrier Ryan got. Why wasn't Joy leaning in the door frame, helping him deal with this? Didn't she understand that, in her desire to make everybody else happy, she'd backed away from them? Once more, she'd left a doorway empty and edged into the shadows of a hallway, telling herself it was for the best, that it was what other people wanted.

But what about last night? Ryan wanted to shout. How could he and Joy get married again and raise kids together if she was still hiding in hallways? Waiting in the wings?

Suddenly that empty doorway came to represent everything that had gone wrong in their marriage.

You'd better face it, Ryan. She's not ready.

This morning, on the drive here, while *he* was deciding how to deal with *her* estranged daughter, Joy was wringing her hands in the car wondering: What was Elayne thinking? Feeling? How would Elayne handle their plans to get married again? Was she going to be okay with it?

At first glance—to a stranger, say—Joy's voiced concern would seem natural. In fact, Joy *was* nice. The nicest person Ryan had ever met. It was why he'd married her. But now he knew the pitfalls, which was why, in the car, he'd turned an echoed, "Is *Elayne* going to be okay with our marriage?"

Joy had glanced at him in surprise. "Don't you want her to be happy?"

Of course. But that wasn't the point. Ryan had tightly gripped the steering wheel, reining in his temper, and was glad when his voice stayed level. Too bad he couldn't fight the irony. "Us getting married again should work out well for the *kids*."

Joy had entirely missed his barb. "It will," she'd said, nodding.

What about how it'll work out for *us?* he'd wanted to scream. "Don't *you* want to marry me?" But even then, he'd known it was no use. Some things never changed. Some *people* never changed.

"I don't care what you say," Elayne started in again sullenly. "I'm staying with you, Uncle Ryan."

Ryan turned from the empty doorway to Elayne, his heart aching for Joy, since he was sure she was overhearing this. It was such a shame. Joy's misguided need to do whatever her thirteen-year-old daughter wanted simply marked the depth of her love. When she was his wife, Joy had tried to please him in the exact same way.

"I can come to California, right?" Elayne ventured, her voice rising. "After what she did, you can't expect me to live with her! She doesn't even care about me! When Aunt May died, she hardly even visited."

"You asked her not to."

Elayne ignored the truth of that. Christy was watching with rapt attention. "If you don't want me to live with you," Elayne continued, "I'll find some other place. I have money now."

Ryan raised an eyebrow.

"They said Aunt May left me everything. I could

get my own apartment." Elayne's chin suddenly quivered. "If you don't want me."

"You're thirteen. You can't get an apartment. And you know it's not a question of wanting you, Elayne."

"Then I'm coming to L.A."

Christy scooted closer to Elayne. "I'm gonna come with Elayne," she announced loyally, "'cause she's my sister."

But Christy looked miserable. Before this past week, she'd never been away from her mother more than a night. Clearly she wanted a sister and an extended family, but she'd never experienced the pull of torn loyalites.

Ryan's voice gentled. "You don't want to go back to Mommy's?"

Christy swallowed hard, then shook her head, her wide eyes glazing with tears. "Not if Elayne won't come."

Ryan noticed that Elayne's hand slid down, found Christy's and squeezed. He was grateful for that at least. Elayne liked Christy, which meant she didn't feel alienated from them all.

Elayne said, "So, can we live with you, Uncle Ryan?"

Before he could say no, that they first needed to work things out with their mother, Joy stepped into the empty doorway. "Yes," she said, her voice shaking with emotion over the rejection and her eyes red-rimmed from the tears she'd shed silently in the hallway. "If that's what you two want. If that's what you think will make you happy—'' Her green tear-glistened eyes searched Elayne's. "Will it make you happy?"

"Very," Elayne answered, her voice strained.

When Joy turned her gaze to him, Ryan's jaw dropped in astonishment. The fury he felt brought him to his feet. "So, now you're thinking that you'll stay in New York," he said, his voice low. "While I stay in L.A. with the girls, since that'll make *them* happy?"

Joy's helpless eyes said, "What else can we possibly do right now?"

"I can't believe this," he muttered. Joy was really going to back out of a marriage that she wanted and let go of her own children—all just to please *them!* But why should it surprise him? He knew things hadn't changed. Why had he done the same thing—and expected different results?

"I just want everybody to be happy," Joy whispered miserably, her gaze roving over him, with all the hunger and love in the world.

"Oh, we're a happy bunch," he growled, staring at Joy, not giving a damn that the kids were there. "Joy, I need a wife. A *partner.*"

Shakily she leaned against the door frame for support, her words catching with regret. "I want that, too, Ryan. So much."

Then tell me you're marrying me. That nothing can come between us. That we—you and me—rule the roost. That we make the decisions for our kids.

"What do you want me to do?" she nearly wailed.

Even though he fought it, his voice rose. "What do *you* want to do?"

Her confusion broke his heart. "Why do you always ask me that?"

Because I can't stare through one more empty doorway, Joy, wishing you were there. Sure, she wanted to be his partner. She always had. But that was the hell of it. Joy simply didn't know how.

Chapter Ten

It doesn't matter what you want. You're doing the right thing. "So, why can't he understand?" Joy brooded, hurriedly refolding Christy's sundresses and neatly placing them in a carry-on, the same one Joy had packed last week for Christy to take to California. "He really hasn't changed," she snarled, saying what she'd never say to his face. "He's still the same old self-centered Ryan Holt."

But he's not, Joy. Be fair. He's willing to help raise both girls, not just Christy. She sighed. That's what hurt the most. Ryan was such a good man. Fundamentally. But when it came to day-to-day living, he sometimes saw only one thing—what *he* wanted. He was only angry about how she was handling this situation because he wanted their remarriage so badly.

Well, so did she. But Joy also knew she couldn't always have her way. Lord knew, when her parents died, she'd learned that. She'd rolled with the punches, too. Within a year, she'd been living with Parisian strangers—and she'd learned to bend, to be accommodating and fit in. Yes, Ryan wanted his way. Not that Joy was overly worried about how that self-absorption would affect the girls. Maggie Holt would make sure their emotional needs were met.

And Joy would always be available...

If the girls ever called.

Joy reached, and her hand stilled on a pair of shorts. Suddenly she imagined Ryan and the girls, standing at the small airport where Joy had landed two days ago. How could she say goodbye to them? *You'll just do it, that's how. If their plane leaves before yours, you'll go and see them off. After you've said goodbye, you'll calmly turn away....*

But I can't!

"You're twenty-seven," she muttered. "You can. And you can learn to live without a lot of things." Even Ryan. Hadn't she done so for the past eight months? *Think of it as practice.*

Maybe Ryan couldn't understand, but all Joy cared about right now was Elayne. And if Christy would be happier with her sister, Joy could handle it. Maybe if Elayne lived with Ryan for a while, she'd be happy, but Joy definitely wasn't imposing herself on her daughter, not if it made her miserable. Joy simply couldn't stand it. She'd approach Elayne later, after the girl had a chance to finish grieving for May and when Elayne was acclimated to a new school and friends...

But what if that time doesn't come, Joy? Are you

*really willing to sacrifice your own happiness for
hers?*

"Yes," Joy said between clenched teeth. "It's
exactly what I did thirteen years ago. I can do it
again."

And Christy wasn't leaving forever, she reminded herself. Besides—a lump lodged in Joy's
throat—wasn't it only *fair* that Christy spend more
time with her daddy? Hadn't Joy been selfish, keeping her to herself these past eight months? Mightn't
it hurt Christy not to have more male guidance?

Joy's eyes and nose suddenly smarted, burning
with tears. Glancing around in an effort to redirect
her thoughts, her gaze landed on Christy's pet
snake. The two-foot beige-and-black boa was inside
an aquarium, twining around—and almost looking
like—a long stick. Otherwise, the room where
Christy had been sleeping, with its big bed, fire
crackling in the fireplace and two leather wing
chairs, was as cozy as the room Joy had shared with
Ryan last night. Panic washed over her. *I can't
leave him. And I can't give Elayne up a second
time, not even if being around me hurts her.*

And yet Joy would. She had to.

Suddenly, the wind left her chest, and she remembered a fall she'd taken when she was a kid;
she'd tumbled off a fence at a baseball park—a
high, circular green wooden fence, the interior of
which was painted with corporate-sponsorship lo-
gos. She'd never known what caused the fall. One
minute, she and some other kids had been perched

on the fence, overlooking left field; the next, she was on her back. Lying in the long, dry summer grass, with her hands clawing the cool loamy soil, she'd stared dizzily up at the sky through a laced canopy of green-gold tree leaves, fighting panic because she couldn't breathe anymore. She'd sucked and sucked, but it was as if her windpipe had been torn from her throat.

Deep breath, she'd thought. *Deep breath.*

But the air wouldn't come.

That's how she felt now, like she was about to die. When her breath returned—then and now, in a stiletto-sharp inhalation—she really thought her heart might explode.

Or break.

And what was causing her fall this time around? How, in just two days, had she managed to lose her whole family again, and the career she loved? Dammit, where was the long soft grass that was supposed to cushion the blow of having to walk away from Ryan?

"Joy?" Nikki yelled from downstairs.

Deep breath. She wasn't sitting on a fence, she wasn't about to fall. Maybe Ryan had booked their flights, as he'd tersely said he was going to during the return drive to Jon's. Riding in the car had been tense, worse somehow because of Ryan's repeated attempts to find music on a radio they both knew was broken. Maybe that's what these past two days have really been, Joy had thought—me and Ryan, trying to find music on a dead radio, trying to find love when it's long gone.

No one had spoken. When they'd arrived at the house, the back doors were simultaneously flung open and the girls bolted out.

"Joy?" Nikki yelled again.

"Sorry. What do you need?" And why couldn't Ryan be more understanding? Sometimes one's own needs really weren't the most important thing. Couldn't Ryan see Joy had no choice but to put Elayne and Christy first, even if her continued separation from him was tearing her apart?

"Phone's for you," yelled Nikki.

Frowning, Joy reached, stretching over the bed for the phone on the bedside table. At least this wasn't the bed she'd shared with Ryan. She couldn't stand to see the messy covers—not quite yet—even if the next task on her list was to make the bed, so Nikki wouldn't have to. She lifted the receiver.

"Joy, you sneak! I didn't know you had it in you!"

Joy eyes widened with surprise as she sank onto the bed. "Melinda?"

"As I'm sure you've guessed, everybody at SWM's talking about you this morning. I spoke with Mr. Stern before phoning you, and he said he'd call Wylie…. Anyway—let's cut right to the chase, shall we?—SWM wants you on the next flight back."

Joy's heart thudded with relief. She needed this

job, especially if Elayne was going to be living with Ryan; she couldn't let Ryan pay Elayne's expenses. Since he was taking the girls, he was going to need another place, too, maybe a house. *Yes, a house. No more apartments. I could give him the money.* That way, Christy could have a yard to play in, and Elayne could have a private room to decorate exactly as she pleased. The idea warmed Joy.

"Joy?"

"Yes, I'm here." Because it felt too good to be true, Joy fought the urge to ask if there was a hitch to Melinda's offer. Melinda usually had an unstated agenda, and often by the time Joy figured it out, it was too late. What had prompted Melinda to change her mind?

"I take it you're speechless?"

Joy's fingers tightened around the handset, and she readjusted the coiled line, standing and walking around the bed so the cord wouldn't have to stretch so far. "Actually I am. You were saying you want me back?"

"Are you kidding?" Melinda enthused. "As soon as I got into the office this morning—"

"You're in the office on the day after Christmas?"

"Absolutely. The work doesn't stop just because of a holiday, you know." Melinda paused for effect. "Anyway, Jon called first thing this morning with the news. He said you're an absolute inspiration, and that you've single-handedly convinced him to write for SWM again."

Joy's lips parted in silent protest. Jon had already

written the story—it was right here on the bed, its few loose sheets bound in a plastic protective binder. During the long wait yesterday, while they'd been looking for the kids, Joy had told Jon why she'd initially come here, explaining that even though she was unemployed, she'd be happy to hand-deliver his manuscript in New York. Feeling too guilty about her intrusion in his life to follow through on her initial plans, Joy had told him she was only sorry she would no longer be working with him.

Apparently Jon had other ideas.

"After talking to Jon," Melinda was saying, "and after hearing more about his long-term goals, which involve writing series books for adolescents that we hope compete with R.L. Stein's, we're just *praying* you'll come home to SWM, Joy."

Home? Joy thought. "Praying?" she said aloud. Wasn't that a little strong? Melinda believed in one law on earth—her own. The image of her and the company brass praying for anything, especially something so insignificant as Joy's return, was so ludicrous that Joy actually smiled, if grimly.

"Now, you don't have to answer immediately," said Melinda. "I just want to know if we can expect you in my office…"

Unexpected anger boiled up inside Joy as Melinda continued rambling in that put-on perky voice. *Have I lost my mind?* Joy thought. *Am I really going back?*

"…tomorrow at eight-thirty sharp, Joy? That

way, we can discuss SWM's formal offer. I hope you're as excited as I am. I always said you were one of our most prized assets.''

And when would you have said that, Melinda? Two days ago when you fired me?

''Just like I always said,'' Melinda went on, ''you're a real trooper!''

''Thanks, Melinda.'' *Steady old faithful, that's me,* she thought. Trouble was, Joy suddenly felt as if she was going to blow like a geyser.

Sighing, Joy tamped down the emotion. As Melinda continued extolling her virtues, Joy took in the new sundresses and shorts that she'd bought for Christy to take to L.A. Joy had usually eaten at her desk, but she'd taken some rare lunch hours to choose the clothes. If Christy hadn't loved them, Joy would have returned the items the next day, and tried again. She'd wanted Christy to feel great when she saw her dad again.

There's nothing I won't do to please my girls.

Feeling heartsick, she reminded herself that the SWM salary would allow her to visit L.A. frequently. Slowly, maybe she could make things right between herself and Elayne, and then maybe she and Ryan really could get back together…

Then she could leave SWM.

''Eight-thirty?'' Melinda prompted.

Joy mustered enthusiasm. ''Great! I'll be there.''

Hanging up, she turned and realized that Ryan was standing in the doorway, still looking furious. *The man definitely knows how to take up his space,* she thought. She had to give him that. He wasn't large—five foot nine and tightly muscled—but he was so focused, so commanding and self-assured, that he seemed to fill the door frame completely. He'd shaved, combed back his hair and changed into other clothes at the inn—cuffed maroon wool slacks that hugged his narrow hips, and a black sweater that made his eyes look darker than they really were. Right now those eyes looked like two hot coals. They were full of censure and searing into her.

Involuntarily Joy rested her hand on the phone receiver again to brace herself. She hated when they were fighting. In fact, Joy couldn't stand discord of any kind. Anything other than harmony made her so uncomfortable that she'd do anything to set things right. Especially now, since the knowing look in his eyes was so unsettling.

His voice was low, sounding almost lazy because of his heightened efforts to control his temper; his tone carried faint accusation. "Done packing for Christy?"

It was the last thing Joy expected him to say. She squinted. "What's wrong with me packing for Christy?"

"She's eight. She could do most of this herself."

"But..."

"I know. You don't mind. You're her mother." Ryan's eyes strayed to the bed. "Just hurry. We need to be out of here in under an hour. I got flights at nearly the same time, but we have to swing back by the inn for your rental car.''

Joy panicked. Under an hour? ''So soon?''

Uttering a soft grunt of frustration, Ryan threw up his hands. ''What exactly did you want to stick around here for?''

She felt stung. She guessed nothing. But his tone was so angry, so abrupt—as if they'd spent the last twenty-four hours engaged in some unpleasant business that was now thankfully concluded. ''What about Noodles?''

''Don't you worry, Joy,'' he chided softly, a slight smile playing on his mouth though he wasn't really amused. ''Noodles will be fine. In fact, we'll *all* be fine. Jon and Nikki will make sure Noodles gets shipped. We don't have enough time to get a crate and pack him properly.''

''I hate to impose. Maybe we could stay and—''

''Stay here because of a snake?'' Ryan's eyes drifted over her as if to say *you would.* ''Besides, I know you're anxious to get back to SWM.''

She fought the humiliated color that rose in her cheeks. ''I don't have a choice but to go back. It's for the kids, so I can send you money.''

''Oh?'' He raised an eyebrow. ''So you didn't even come here to get your job back for *you,* but for the kids.''

In spite of herself, she was starting to shake with anger. ''Please,'' she said, somehow keeping her voice even. ''You know I don't like confrontations.'' She hadn't raised her voice, and already, her heart was beating too hard and her face felt red. It was hard to breathe.

"I don't like them, either."

"You thrive on them!" she sputtered.

He was still lazily leaning in the doorway. Only his eyes—narrowed and darkened to black—gave away his anger. That, and the agitated hand he thrust through his hair, pushing it from his forehead. His voice remained controlled. "That's where you're wrong, Joy. I really don't."

Right. That was why, whenever she needed to stand up to people, Ryan rescued her—hounding building superintendents to fix things, calling utility companies about overcharges. He'd even gone to talk to one of her college professors when she thought she deserved an *A,* instead of a *B.* Ryan had taken all her supporting evidence and gotten her the *A,* too.

He surveyed her for a long moment, and when he spoke his voice was cool. "Have you ever paused to consider why you don't like confrontation?"

Her eyes widened. "I guess you're going to tell me."

"Yeah. I think I am."

Sharp breath. She inhaled as he pushed off the door frame, then strode toward her so purposefully that she shrank back, somehow wedging herself in the space where the bedside table met the mattress. He stopped in front of her.

She stared at him. "What?"

He sighed. And suddenly, she decided this new Ryan Holt was even more intimidating than the old one. He was angry—that was plain from his eyes—but he really did have iron-tight control. She could feel the sheer force of his will emanating from him. Without a word, he hooked a finger in the waistband of her slacks, as if she might run away from what he had to say. She could feel his knuckles against her belly, through her shirt, and it wasn't nearly as unpleasant as she wished it was.

"What?" she repeated calmly, feeling absolutely determined to stand up to him this time. "Now that you've had a crash course with Laura, you're going to pychoanalyze me?"

"No," he said, edging close enough that she could feel his breath. "But when you lost your parents, I think you were just as worried as Elayne is now. You were about her age, but instead of reacting by being angry and defensive, I imagine you just tried to please everybody, as best you could. Deep down, you were scared your aunt and uncle would run out on you. That they'd die, too, or just quit loving you. Since you knew you were too young to take care of yourself, you bent over backward, trying to make people love you, always terrified that if you voiced your own needs, you'd be perceived as a nuisance."

With the words, his breath kept coming, and she was conscious of it on her cheek and lips, and of the pulse beat in her throat, and of the seeming silence around them. "Nice theory," she whispered, wishing her throat wasn't so dry.

His face was impassive. "Thanks."

As usual, he was right on the money, but she didn't expect to feel so much anger. At times such as this, qualities she admired in him turned on her—his perceptive intelligence being among them. Her words were stiff. "Anyway, what's this got to do with us?"

His eyes widened and he loosed another tight-lipped sigh of frustration. "Everything."

"Why can't you understand?" she suddenly burst out, wishing she had the nerve to simply push him away, because being with him and so near the bed brought unwanted thoughts about the intimacy they could no longer share. "I don't have a choice!"

"That's you," he chided softly. "The poor little victim."

"I want to go to L.A.," she raged, ignoring him. "I want to be with you, Ryan—" Her voice broke and her eyes started to plead. She pointed past him, toward the empty doorway. "Those are my girls down there, my babies! I want to be with them. I want—"

"Then why *aren't* you?"

At his sudden shout, she gave a little start—a jump, really—then flinched again from the aftershock. A second later, she realized her heart was pounding too hard because they were right back where they'd been eight months ago, just before he'd left. Her voice, when she found it, came out strained. "I'm doing what I think is right."

"The way I see it, you're just letting a couple of kids railroad you, Joy. That's how afraid you are that they won't love you. But right now, Elayne needs parents. A regimen. Rules. She needs to know that someone's going to punish her if she comes in past curfew."

"Fine! Solve it with rules and punishments. But I think she needs what she says she needs—space and understanding. *That's* love, Ryan."

He stared at her. "Is it?" he said softly. And then without another word, he dropped his hold on her, turned and headed for the door.

She gaped at his retreating back. Why couldn't he get it through his thick skull? She knew exactly how Elayne felt. Ryan had been right about that much. Like Elayne, Joy had feared she'd be alone.

And now I am *alone!*

Vaguely she wondered if this wasn't some self-fulfilling prophecy. Some subconscious playing out of the things she most feared. Then she snapped to her senses. "Ryan!"

When he didn't turn, Joy started after him, grabbing his biceps, forcing him to turn around. He stared at her, the judgment in his eyes making her sorry she'd so uncharacteristically pursued him. But she'd make him understand. She had to. "I love you so much, Ryan. All I want is for us to be together. But I have to do what I think is right."

She was prepared for another show of his temper,

but not the bleak despair that somehow managed to fill both his eyes and yet made them look empty. "You'll never change, Joy."

In the silence, the fire crackled, and she became aware of muted voices sounding from downstairs. Her throat was closing tight, but she managed to repeat, "I have to do what I think is right."

He nodded. "We need to leave in forty-five minutes." With that, he simply turned and headed down the hallway.

Staring at his retreating back—at his muscular shoulders and the manly sway of his narrow hips— Joy suddenly brought her hands to her chest, pressing both palms there as if Ryan was something small she'd once held in her hand. She pressed her heart hard—as if by doing so, she could keep Ryan there forever.

But she didn't follow him.

"WELL…" Joy swallowed audibly, nervously tying the belt of her long black coat, then leaning—for support, it seemed—on the extended handle of a rolling carry-on. "Guess your flight leaves a few minutes after mine."

So, now they were going to do small talk. Ryan shoved his hands deep into his pockets. Fine. He could do small talk. "Looks that way."

"There's some bad weather," she said. "Snow. Some of the flights out of Charlotte got grounded."

"You don't say?" Ryan nodded, then glanced around the area where they were standing, mostly since looking at Joy was making his temper flare. Between the two gates were rows of seats, and on the other side of the metal detectors was a long hallway. A decorated pine tree was near the front doors; the shop windows were sprayed with canned snow. The kids were slumped sullenly in chairs a few feet away.

"You're Gate B?" Joy said.

As if she didn't know. "Right. And you're Gate A."

"There're only two gates."

That was Joy, always quick on the uptake. "Right."

When she fell silent, his lips compressed. He really couldn't believe this. Was Joy actually walking away from him and the kids? When he looked at her again, slow fury such as he hadn't felt in months—the same kind of uncontrollable fury Ryan never wanted to feel again—slowly spread through him.

At least this time, the anger was mostly directed at himself. He'd been such a fool to hope. And damn if—even now—he hadn't stopped. He was thinking maybe—just maybe—Joy would suddenly tell them all to go to hell, that she was coming to L.A. Or that he'd glance up, once he and the kids boarded, to see her taking the seat beside him.

Just like in the movies.

A voice came over a loudspeaker. "We'd like to invite all passengers to board at Gate A now."

Joy swallowed hard, glancing toward the gate. "That's me."

"Sounds like it." Suddenly, his heart ached as he saw a barely discernible maternal lift of Joy's arm, that age-old invitation to be hugged. Her voice raised, trembled. "Bye, kids."

Neither even looked up. Christy's arms were clenched tightly over her chest, and she stared straight down at the floor. Elayne pointedly shifted her eyes toward the metal detectors.

Joy's voice was strangled. "I'll ship Christy's things."

Ryan thought he'd explode. After eight years of mothering Christy, Joy was simply going to get on a plane, walk away, and ship her child's belongings across the country?

Suddenly turning, feeling unspeakably outraged, Ryan glared at the kids. "Get up," he growled. "Both of you. Hug your mother goodbye." Slowly, sullenly, they began to rise to their feet, but Joy was turning away. He grabbed her elbow. "Can't you at least hug them goodbye, Joy?"

"They don't want—"

"Who gives a damn what they want!" he shouted.

Heads turned.

"And dammit—" Ryan suddenly paused, shutting his eyes. *Deep breath*. When he opened his eyes again, they felt gritty with tears. "I'm sorry, Joy," he said hoarsely, his voice breaking with defeat because all day, he'd been on the verge of los-

ing his temper, "but I just don't want to yell anymore."

Ryan glanced toward the girls, who were standing uncertainly near the chairs, as he released Joy's
arm. "Go ahead," he said, his voice softening with
regret as she turned to go. "Walk away. But if you
ever get it, Joy, give us a call."

Chapter Eleven

Trails of fog looped around the receding airport like strings, slowly shrouding it, and as the plane lifted, snow clouds came between Joy and the mountains, turning the pines a milky gray-green before obscuring them completely. And then Joy couldn't see anything.

Deep breath.

No matter how many she took, it didn't help. Like a smoke screen, a wall of gray had been thrown up in front of her, and Ryan and the girls would always be on the other side.

"Would you like to trade seats?"

Blinking, she glanced beside her at the affluent-looking elderly man in the window seat. His eyes were young for his years—perceptive blue eyes that invited confidences. "No. But thanks for asking."

Discouraging further conversation, Joy unlatched the drink tray, brought Jon's plastic-bindered manuscript from her lap and opened it. Despite her mood, or maybe because of a desire to escape, or because Jon Sleet had a gift and could weave magic spells around readers, young or old, Joy actually felt a spark of interest.

"It was years since little Jenny had gone away," began the story.

Even the opening words pulled at Joy's heart, since she knew Jenny was the name of the daughter Jon had lost, the one for whom he used to write all his Christmas stories. Glancing through the window again, Joy felt a sudden connection between herself and Jon—as if, through all the clouds, they were holding two ends of the same string.

After all, she'd just lost her girls, too—Christy who was only steps from puberty. Elayne, whose headstrong defiance—that practiced scowl and menacing earring—did so little to hide the beautiful woman she was becoming. As soon as next year, men might start to look at her, their heads turning as Elayne passed on the street—tossing her blond mane, sweeping her challenging green eyes past them, as teenage girls did, pretending to be unaware men even existed.

And I might not be there to see her grow.

Joy forced her attention to the story again, which was about how a man had lost his wife and his daughter, Jenny, in an ice storm. Because the storm was terrifying and fierce, with whipping winds that ripped down power lines, felled trees and leveled homes, the man hid inside his huge stone house, while ice wound in ribbons on the curving roads and icicles rained down from the gutters like daggers. The man could only hope for the safe return of his wife and daughter, who were out visiting.

But they never returned.

After that, the man became so cold and hate-filled that his heart froze, just like the ice he'd hidden from. Everything he touched turned to ice: the walls of his house were solid sheets of ice, and the blooms in his garden froze on their stalks.

No one in Holiday Hamlet went near the ice castle, which seemed tainted by tragedy. The few who tried—mostly schoolchildren on a dare—couldn't get close because the frozen blades of grass around the man's house cut their feet, even through their sneakers.

"You'd better watch out," the townsfolk warned. "If that man touches you, you'll turn into an ice statue." It was even rumored that behind the house, out in the garden where no one went anymore, there were, indeed, such statues—of snoopers who had come too close.

But one day, a little girl named Christmas came to visit, treading very lightly and using specially made shoes that protected her feet. *Christmas.* When she saw her daughter's name, Joy's hand stilled on the page, a lump forming in her throat.

And then she read on, about how, for the twelve days of Christmas, the little girl brought the man gifts. She brought fire in a bronze bucket, trying to melt him, and used an ice pick to carve holiday messages on his writing tablets, which were now made of ice. But it wasn't until Christmas morning that the little girl did the unthinkable—and kissed the man.

Oh, she was afraid she'd freeze into an ice statue.

But instead the man began to magically melt, along with everything else in his house. Even though it was Christmas morning, and cold in Holiday Hamlet, a soft yellow light suffused the whole town from the warmth of the man's home. Leaning down—the man could do so now because his knees were no longer frozen stiff—he took Christmas's hand and together, they walked down the mountain…

If you ever get it, give us a call.

Ryan's words came from nowhere just as Joy's hand stilled on the last page, right over where Jon Sleet had typed The End. Was Ryan right? Was there such a thing as too much love? Maybe. Too much—or at least the loss of it for someone who had loved too much—had turned a man to ice and frozen his heart.

Was Joy hiding the way he had? Running away?

If so, it was no wonder the girls had run away from home. What if Joy didn't turn around now? Who would show them how to take a stand?

Dammit, she thought. She'd been right to give up Elayne. It had hurt Joy more than it had hurt Elayne, who had never even known. At sixteen, grieving for her own parents, Joy had had absolutely nothing to offer her daughter, but Aunt May and Uncle Jer did. So, why was Joy buying into

Elayne's version of things? Just how far was Joy willing to go to ensure that people loved her back?

Sudden anger unfurled in her. Not this far.

What do you want, Joy?

She wasn't even sure anymore. Was she as frozen inside as the iceman? Empty inside?

But no. Because she thought: I want to marry Ryan. I want to mother my kids. I want to take a family trip to Beckley, lay flowers on May's and Jer's graves, and let them know how sorry I am that we spent so much time apart, then I want to visit my parents' graves, too, because I haven't been there for so long. She wanted to know what kind of flowers were growing there and to plant some perennials.

And there were other things, less serious things.

Like getting something brighter to wear. She was sick of wearing what so many New Yorkers did— basic black. Maybe she'd get something yellow. Sunburst yellow. And she'd start gardening again. She missed sinking to the elbows in muddy soil and imagining how the flowers would look when they bloomed, the way she always imagined how Christy and Elayne would look as they grew.

Oh, she wanted—

So much.

"THE PRODIGAL RETURNS!" exclaimed Melinda from the far end of the hallway. Somehow, from here, Melinda seemed like a blur. Everything about her—the trim brown bob, standard-issue pearls and black suit—seemed to blend together. Suddenly there seemed nothing unique about Melinda Keen, nothing distinguishing. Her outfit did exactly what it was meant to—made her fade into the swarming crowds of midtown Manhattan office workers.

"Coffee's waiting in my office!" Melinda enthused.

As if Joy were a visiting power broker, not the woman Melinda fired two days ago. *Deep breath,* Joy thought. SWM was already a slice of the past. She'd intended to tell Melinda exactly what she could do with the job, but first she'd have a little fun. After all, she deserved it. Smiling, Joy tucked Jon Sleet's manuscript more tightly under her arm, skirted the reception desk and headed down the oriental runner as faces popped out of doorways—the same doorways they'd ducked into two days ago as Joy was being escorted from the building.

"Good work, Joy!" said Claire from the art department, sipping her coffee. "Congratulations on getting Jon Sleet back."

That she really hadn't was too much to explain, so Joy merely nodded.

"Well, let's get right down to it!" Melinda said, urging Joy inside her office and indicating that she should seat herself in an armchair facing the desk. "You'll be editing Jon, of course. And you can have your old office back."

"You're kidding?" Joy couldn't help but say, ignoring the coffee Melinda's assistant had poured. "You mean no one's moved into it yet?"

Melinda laughed as if that was the funniest joke she'd ever heard. "Okay—" She smiled a beaming smile. "You can move into the empty corner office."

Of course. Melinda would think Joy was simply holding out for more. It's what Melinda would do under the circumstances. "Please, Melinda," Joy began.

But sensing her resistance, Melinda plunged on, now offering a decorating budget for the new office. When Joy could get a word in edgewise, she said, "Really, Melinda, I—"

"Your salary's being adjusted," Melinda interrupted. "And you'll get a new title. If you really want it, I don't see why we can't bring you into our stock options program…"

When the phone rang, Melinda winced. "I'm so sorry," she apologized, pursing her lips and shaking her head. "I *told* the front desk to hold all my calls." She lifted the receiver. "Oh? The call's for Joy. It's her *daughter?*" Melinda flashed Joy a winning smile. "Then of course we'll take it!"

As Melinda handed over the receiver, she murmured, "If I haven't mentioned it, I admire you so much for juggling parenthood and a career. Let me take this opportunity to say how anxious we are to accommodate your parental duties when you come back on board with flex time…"

Joy didn't bother to listen to the rest. Who knew what Melinda really thought? She blew with the wind, voicing no real opinions or desires, only saying whatever was most politic. Two days ago, Joy lacked initiative. Today, she was the prodigal returned. Not that Joy blamed the woman. It had gotten her where she wanted to go.

"Hello?"

"*¡Ola, señorita! ¿Qué pasa?*"

Hearing Christy's voice made Joy's heart pound. "Hey there, sweetheart," she said, leaning closer to Melinda's desk so the cord reached more easily. Lifting the coiled wire, she untangled it from an in-box as Christy plunged into conversation.

"Sorry to call you at work, but it's boring here."

Joy smiled, knowing this was a lead-in to something else. The catch in Christy's voice indicated that she hadn't called solely because she missed her mom. "You don't like L.A.?"

"We're not even *in* L.A.!"

Joy's eyes narrowed, her heart skipping a beat. Had something gone wrong? "No?"

"No! Our plane got grounded 'cause of snow. And so we came back to the inn. And now Dad and Elayne decided we're gonna live here, which is okay because Pam and Hub need help running the inn that Dad bought. This way I can see Jon and Nikki and learn how to ride horses."

"What?" Joy shrieked. "Your dad's going to run the inn?"

"I don't know, Mom! When I asked him, he said he bought it for sentimental reasons 'cause that's where you and him got back together. He said he wasn't ever going to bring in strippers—"

"Strip malls," Joy said, correcting her.

"Like, uh, whatever," Christy continued, her words a testament to her new sister's influence. "Anyway, the inn's real neat. But it's so big that Daddy put some ads in the paper for helpers. We gotta get cooks and laundry people. And some guys to put on a new roof. Not that I care about that, but I'm calling because I'm so worried about Elayne."

Joy felt suddenly breathless. Maybe at the mention of Elayne. Or because of why Ryan had bought the inn. Had he really done so because that's where the warmth of their marriage was rekindled? Her heart swelled with emotion. "What?" she said, suddenly shaking her head and trying to keep up with Christy's monologue.

"I said I'm worried because Elayne needs a mom. She's gonna be in big trouble when school starts after Christmas. Especially since there's no one to take her shopping for school clothes, and she won't take that earring out of her eyebrow. She's got to make all new friends, and without a mom, how's she gonna—"

"You don't need a mom, huh?" Joy interjected, sudden tears tugging at her eyes. "I mean, you'll be starting a new school, too."

Christy's voice hitched. "Oh, no, I'm fine. It's just that Elayne messed up one of my new dresses when she did the laundry, and when she showed me how to load the dishwasher, I broke a real nice plate. Mrs. Scudder can't work in the garden this spring either because of arthritis, and Elayne says she doesn't know anything about flowers. Elayne's a pretty good sister, but she really needs…''

''Needs?'' Joy prodded.

''Guidance,'' Christy said after a moment, trying on a new grown-up word.

Joy had to fight down a soft chuckle. ''I see,'' she said. And looking around Melinda's office, she really did see. She didn't want to be in a world where attitudes were never true and alliances had no permanence. ''Hmm,'' Joy murmured, toying with the phone cord. ''I guess you're getting me a little worried here, Christy.''

Christy giggled. ''I am?''

''Of course you are.'' It was exactly why her daughter had called. ''I mean, who's going to talk Elayne into taking that earring out of her eyebrow?''

''I don't know, Mom! She won't listen to me, 'cause I'm just a sister! And Dad's just a boy. And Mr. and Mrs. Scudder are too old. But maybe Elayne would listen to a—''

''Mom?'' finished Joy. ''Well, in that case, I guess I'd better hurry up and get over there, huh?''

Christy sighed heavily. ''Could you?''

''Only if you'll keep it a secret. Can you do that?''

''Excited hop!'' Christy squealed. ''I sure can!''

Joy was still smiling when she hung up the phone. ''Melinda,'' she began. ''I'm really sorry, but I've got to run. I've got another interview.''

''From another publisher?'' Melinda worriedly

clutched her short strand of pearls and leaned forward aggressively. "We'll match any offer."

"Well then let me tell you what I'd like."

When she was done with her demands, Melinda looked flabbergasted. "So you only want freelance work? You'll ensure we get Jon Sleet, but you don't want to work full-time? What other position are you taking?"

Wife.

Mother.

Emotion suddenly caught in Joy's throat. "I don't even know if I can get the position," she found herself saying, scooting up and perching on the edge of the overstuffed chair. "The offer might not still stand." She suddenly smiled. "But there are a number of ads in a little local paper, maybe one's for household help."

Melinda looked vaguely ill. "Excuse me? Are you serious?"

Joy chuckled. "I sure am." She sighed. "Of course, in addition to cooking, cleaning and laundry, I'm hoping these hard taskmasters will let me indulge some of my own interests, such as landscaping."

Melinda was looking at her as if she'd never seen her before, her eyes wide and lips parted in shock. "Well, as long as you're sure we're getting Jon Sleet," she remarked, "I guess I'll just say good luck."

"Thanks, Melinda," said Joy, meaning it.

"SO, YOU'RE GOING TO FIX IT up the way it used to be, Uncle Ryan?" Elayne said.

"Not without your help." Ryan finished his walk around the ballroom, then seated himself on the couch next to Elayne, right where Joy had been seated during the Christmas party.

"Here." Glancing down at the open photo album in Elayne's lap—it was one Pam Scudder had brought down from the attic—Ryan pointed at a sepia-toned picture. "What do you think of re-opening the restaurant, making it look like that again?"

"Cool," Elayne said.

"If the restaurant's French, can I be a waitress, Daddy?" Christy piped in.

Ryan smiled, though his heart wasn't really in it. "If it was Spanish or Greek you wouldn't want to work there, huh?" he teased.

"Non, Papa!" Christy was sitting on the floor in front of the couch, cross-legged in front of the fire, looking at a second album, and seemingly oblivious of the undercurrents of emotion he and Elayne had been battling. Must be nice, he thought, watching her merrily turning pages. The resilience of youth, he decided, had a frightening visage. Didn't she even miss her mother?

Elayne looked miserable. And much less defiant. Yesterday, she'd acted on anger. But today, with Joy gone for good, Elayne felt responsible. If the truth be told, Elayne wasn't all that sorry she hadn't been raised by a struggling, hurting teenager. She was no fool, and knew that May and Jer had given her more than Joy could have. But because she was just a girl, Elayne was having trouble handling all their changing relationships. It didn't help that she knew Ryan and Joy had planned to reconcile. Or that Joy left because she was trying to make Elayne happy.

Looping a paternal arm around Elayne's shoulder, he drew her to his chest. "Deep sigh," he said with a quick wink.

Elayne nodded.

There wasn't any use in saying more. Ryan glanced around—taking in the snow-blanketed hills beyond the window and the decorated Christmas tree—before his gaze settled on the roaring fire. After all the years in New York and L.A., it was strange that this inn—where he'd reconciled with Joy, however temporarily—would become the place where he'd settle. But it felt right to Ryan. Like home.

He and the kids could be of real use here. Pam and Hub were "rarin'," as they put it, to move into a caretaker's cottage on the property, so Ryan and the girls could have the house. With rooms to spare, his parents could come dote on the grandkids anytime they wanted. Ryan could even host the Holt family reunions.

He gazed at Elayne again. With time, her wounds would heal. Already, he'd sat the girls down and talked things out as best he could. Elayne's sense of betrayal wouldn't leave overnight. But he'd carefully explained how Joy was. How she hadn't walked away from Elayne yesterday because she didn't want her—but because she had trouble standing up for her own needs and desires. Ryan was pretty sure Elayne understood, even if she looked as raw and shaky as he felt.

Not that Ryan wanted Joy back.

If he did, he'd simply pack up the girls, hop on a plane and move back into their old apartment. Yeah, Ryan still knew how to take what he wanted. But he didn't want Joy in his life unless she really changed.

"Given how depressed you three look—"

Ryan's head came up as the female voice continued, "—a little household help won't do you any good. Maybe I should turn right back around and go home."

Joy was standing in the doorway and Ryan couldn't tear his eyes from her. He barely registered that Christy was squealing and jumping to her feet.

"Excited hop! I knew she was coming!"

That explained why Christy hadn't been the least depressed, Ryan thought, feeling his throat close. Framed in the doorway—beneath a hanging sprig of mistletoe, he now realized—Joy looked like a picture. Completely familiar, but different in a way he couldn't figure out—until he realized she was wearing a buttery yellow zippered jacket instead of her good black coat. Shiny blue plastic gardening clogs were on her feet, and a wooden caddy was in hand, brimming with tools—trowels, weeders, hand spades and a watering can and rubber gloves.

His eyes trailing over her, Ryan understood what she was saying. That the woman he married was back. She'd gotten a little lost along the way, but she was now standing in the doorway she'd left empty for so long. She was ready to get down to the nitty gritty, to the soil of their lives, to fix things and make them grow.

Elayne's sullen words came out of the blue. "I thought you got your old job back."

His breath caught in unspoken warning. Surely the words would send Joy running back out the door.

But Joy didn't miss a beat. "Oh," she said lightly, still smiling, leaning carelessly in the doorway, even if the unusual brightness of her eyes said she knew how important this moment was. "As a matter of fact, Elayne, I did get my old job back."

"So why aren't you there?"

"Deep sigh," sighed Joy. "It was quite the offer, too, I assure you. Corner office. More travel. Why, I believe Melinda even mentioned Europe. And then there was the salary hike and the stock options and the expense account. I guess I'll miss having lunch in all the swanky places where you get to glimpse famous people."

Elayne's voice rose. "Like, uh, we didn't ask you to come here! So, why don't you go back!"

"Because, well..." Joy's eyes settled on Ryan's, her gaze feeling as warm as the buttery jacket she wore. "Because a little girl named Christmas called to tell me about a want ad in the *Holiday Hamlet Register,* and I'd like to interview. Because I think I'd rather help put on a new roof, and be a landscaper and—" Joy drew in a sudden, choked sound. "And a wife and mother."

That was all it took.

Ryan forgot the kids and crossed the room, reaching the doorway where he knew his wife would be from now on. Christy was on his heels, and Elayne followed, stopping a few paces away. Catching Ryan in her arms first, Joy let a tear roll down her cheek, and by the time she'd included Christy in her embrace, more tears were falling freely.

"Ryan," she whispered. "I'll do whatever it takes."

"So will I," he whispered back, cupping her chin quickly and fastening his mouth to hers. "This time, I promise we'll get it right."

Nodding, she tore her eyes from his and looked at Elayne, who was hanging back. "What they offered me was just a job, Elayne," she said. "But only you can offer me a daughter. What I want most is to be your mother."

Ryan's heart hammered. This was the Joy he needed beside him. The woman who could be his partner and chase the dreams they shared. His arms curled tighter around her, a hand slipping around her neck and ruffling her hair as she lifted her arm—throwing it open wide, inviting Elayne into the group hug.

Elayne didn't move.

And strangely, Ryan knew it didn't matter. Maybe Joy didn't even expect Elayne to come. All that mattered right now was that Joy had extended her love. From there on out, it was for Elayne to decide.

"Please," Joy whispered, not giving up.

All their eyes fastened on Elayne—his, Joy's, Christy's—and then, as if pulled by the strength of their joined gazes, Elayne slowly moved forward. The four tentative steps it took to find her mother's arms felt like miles, but then Elayne was hugging her mother, swaying with Ryan and Christy.

"Deep sigh," Joy whispered.

Ryan found her eyes, then caught her chin with his fingertips once more. God, how he'd missed her smile. Nothing in the world—not city lights nor Christmas glitter—could sparkle like these crystal eyes that were glossed with tears. "Excited hop," Ryan whispered softly, pressing his forehead to Joy's, then ducking his head down so he could take another kiss. "But I warn you, I'm not the kind who'll live in sin."

"Don't worry," she whispered huskily. "My intentions are noble. I'll make an honest man of you, Ryan."

"When?"

"Soon," Joy assured, her lips parting for another tender sweep of his. As his mouth closed more tightly over hers, Ryan's heart swelled, filling with more joy than it ever had. Because even though he'd already married her once, he'd only now found the woman he needed, the woman he loved.

Epilogue

"High heels would look better," Elayne said with pique. She stared nervously through the inn's back door, at where the wedding-goers had gathered in the garden, and then she glared at Joy's feet again. "I know you're pregnant, but it's only for a couple of hours. And flats are so..." Elayne shrugged as if there simply were no words.

Joy sighed with a maternal smile as she smoothed the fabric of her wedding dress over her swollen belly, making the yellow tea-length chiffon dress rise and fall. "This coming from someone who wears earrings in her eyebrows."

"One earring," defended Christy, taking up for her sister. "And she took it out for the wedding."

Elayne actually left the earring out most of the time now, especially since a certain someone—a hockey player from her new school—had started regularly walking her home. Overall, things were going well, Joy thought now. The kids were resettled, with plenty of friends. And no two girls could have looked more beautiful, standing here in their matching white lace dresses.

Oh, Joy and Ryan fought more than they used to. But it was a good kind of fighting—where Joy stood up for what she wanted and got her way at least half the time. Ryan's newfound belief in family counseling had them all talking more openly with each other, and sometimes it felt more like a curse than a blessing. But they were making it.

Deep sigh. Joy stared out at the sprawling gardens, which she was slowly restoring from the old photographs Pam Scudder had provided. It would take years to complete the task, but bright spring blooms were everywhere, including beside the podium where she was about to marry Ryan. Suddenly Joy glanced down at her feet—and the flats that matched her dress. "Are they really terrible?" she suddenly said. "I guess I could have worn heels. It's not every day I get married."

Elayne sighed. "Well, you married Ryan before."

Ryan, Joy noticed, remembering when she'd first heard Elayne drop the word "uncle." Not that Elayne would ever call him Dad. Instead Elayne and Ryan had developed a friendship over these months. They'd become pals, and somehow calling him Ryan seemed only natural.

Not so "Joy." Every time Elayne was forced to call her by name, awkwardness hung in the air. For so long, she'd been "Aunt Joy" and everyone was conscious that "Aunt" had been dropped because,

by rights, Elayne could have called her "Mother."
Joy understood, and was just happy for the close-
ness her daughters—both of them—allowed her to
share.

"And you're getting married five months pregnant," Elayne said with another sigh that sounded
more maternal that most of Joy's own.

"I thought that's when you were supposed to get
married," Christy said, suddenly sounding confused. "I mean, when you get pregnant."

"My, my," Joy chided, "an unwed mother at
my age. What will people think, girls?"

The new Joy Holt had pretty much quit caring.
Oh, not that she wanted to make a spectacle of herself—though Ryan liked to tease her, saying her
brightly colored wardrobe was creating a stir on
North Main Street where, unlike New York where
everyone seemed to wear black, the uniform *du jour*
was faded denim.

"Well," Elayne said, pretending to be much
more perturbed than she really was, "you might not
care, but Christy and I have to go to school around
here."

"Oui, ma soeur!" Christy agreed.

"Maybe we're not the most conventional family
in Holiday Hamlet," Joy conceded, "but you've
got to admit that we have fun." Smiling, she ab-
sently curved her hand over her belly again, and
shook her head in bemusement. What were she and
Ryan thinking, back in December, when they'd

wound up in this town, making love without any protection?

That we wanted to be together again.

Joy smiled. Yes, they'd definitely been thinking that. And she was enjoying this pregnancy so much. With Elayne, she'd been young, frightened and uncertain about the future. With Christy, she and Ryan had been starting out, their heads filled with financial worries. But this pregnancy was plain old fun. It was all about shopping for baby clothes and decorating a nursery.

Joy had never imagined life could be so full. Just like the kids, she had new friends—*real* friends. Nikki was younger than she, but they were enjoying their pregnancies together, since Nikki wasn't but six weeks further along. Joy and Ryan attended birthing classes with the Sleets now, and Christy and Elayne had been in Nikki and Jon's wedding, back in February. Despite her studied air of boredom, Elayne was already begging to baby-sit Nikki's newborn and thrilled about having another new sibling. Playing mama hen gave Elayne a sense of control over her life, which only months before had seemed so precarious.

Business had picked up, too. Jon Sleet's reentry into publishing had brought new tourists into town and, working out of a home office, Joy was editing his and other books. *A Girl Named Christmas* would hit the shelves next holiday season.

Not that Joy was overly concerned with work. She had her hands full with what she liked most—

gardening and taking care of the kids. And loving Ryan. More than anything, that's what was best in her life.

The sudden sound of music brought her from her thoughts.

"You two better get out there," she said to the girls. "We can't get married unless the bridesmaids go first."

"Excited hop!" Christy giggled, running for the door. "C'mon, Elayne!"

"Coming," Elayne said. But she held back. As the door slammed behind Christy, Elayne turned and looked at Joy for a long moment. "Uh…"

Joy raised her eyebrows, her heart filling with love. Her oldest girl was beautiful, breathtakingly so—such a promise of the woman she would no doubt become. Her blond hair was pulled back in a very adult style that showed off pale skin so much like Joy's. "What, Elayne?"

Taking a sudden, nervous step forward, Elayne awkwardly looped her arms around Joy's neck. The hug took Joy by surprise, but she responded, enfolding Elayne in an embrace. "Good luck. The shoes really look cute," Elayne whispered. And after a beat, she added, "Mother."

Before Joy could answer, Elayne had turned and run through the door after Christy, leaving Joy to blink back tears.

"I knew she'd come around."

At Ryan's voice, Joy turned, and as he strode

toward her, she said, "You're supposed to be in the garden, waiting for me—"

Ignoring that, he whisked a handkerchief from his pocket. "Big wince," he said. "We're not even married yet and you're already smearing." Tilting back her head, he dabbed a corner of the handkerchief beneath her eyes, fixing the mascara. "Now don't mess it up again."

Joy smiled, still fighting tears. "She called me Mother."

Ryan pulled her into his arms. "I heard."

"Eavesdropper."

"I like to know what my wife's up to."

"Ex-wife," she stated.

He glanced toward the garden. "Not for much longer."

Her eyes followed his, taking in the flowers. The garden project, she decided, was a lot like her and Ryan's marriage. An excavation, really. Right now, she was chipping away at the old fountains, removing everything that was bad in the foundations. But most of that work was done. Which meant the rest was going to be a wonderful adventure.

"Nervous?" Ryan whispered, pulling her closer.

She chuckled softly—enjoying the feel of his body against hers and hardly caring that a crowd was waiting that included most of Holiday Hamlet, as well as Ryan's parents, siblings, spouses, and all of Elayne and Christy's cousins. His warm hands slid down the sides of her dress, making her voice turn raspy. "I'd be a lot less nervous—" she glanced toward the garden again "—if my fiancé was waiting for me, the way he's supposed to."

Ryan's throaty chuckle made her pulse race. Suddenly she wished the wedding was over and that they were already taking the long weekend they'd planned on the Carolina coast. "Think you've been jilted?" Ryan asked with a sigh, leaning and rubbing his cheek against her neck.

"Maybe."

"Hmm." He delivered a slow kiss. "Want me to marry you?"

"I think you'll do, since it's just a marriage."

He raised an eyebrow. "'Just' a marriage?"

Joy shrugged. "A marriage only takes a few minutes, but I'm offering so much more."

His arched eyebrow raised another fraction. "You've got me interested. I'm listening."

Her eyes strayed outside again, where the musicians—a trio Jon Sleet had recommended—played classical music. Soft strains could be heard through the door. She gazed at the podium where she and Ryan would soon say their vows. And then among the leaves and trees, where more children than they'd planned would probably play, and where, many years from now, surrounded by grandchildren and great-grandchildren, Joy hoped she and Ryan would sit, feeling satisfied with the life they'd made. She pictured them silently holding hands— maybe sitting in the garden gazebo she was going to paint this summer—watching the red Carolina sunsets. Her voice caught as her eyes returned to his. "I'm offering a lifetime, in which to tend to our garden."

"That sounds so good, Joy," said Ryan, his eyes darkening with emotion.

"Good thing," she said huskily.

"Why's that?"

She smiled, her whole body warming as his palms slid another inch over her hips. "Because you're the only man in the world I want to garden with."

"How about one last kiss before we're old married folks again," Ryan suggested throatily. He hugged her tighter and slanted his lips across hers, urging her mouth to open for the honey of his tongue, for a kiss that lasted longer than it ever should have.

And then Ryan simply took her hand, and led her into the garden.

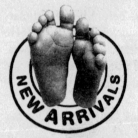

He's every woman's fantasy, but only one woman's dream come true.

Harlequin American Romance brings you THE ULTIMATE...in romance, as our most sumptuous series continues. Because a guy's wealth, looks and bod are nothing without that one special woman.

THE ULTIMATE...

...Catch

#760 *RICH, SINGLE & SEXY*
Mary Anne Wilson
January 1999

...Lover

#762 *A MAN FOR MEGAN*
Darlene Scalera
February 1999

Don't miss any of The Ultimate...series!

Available at your favorite retail outlet.

HARLEQUIN®
Makes any time special ™

COMING NEXT MONTH

#761 SECRET DADDY by Vivian Leiber
Gowns of White
Dr. Corey Harte had wealth, success—but no special lady in his life. There had only ever been one woman: Robyn O'Halloran. It had been four years since their secret night together. Little did he know the secret she carried with her....

#762 A MAN FOR MEGAN by Darlene Scalera
The Ultimate...
Megan Kelly thought she had it all: a steady paycheck, her own house, food on the table. Then there was Gino, who had the commanding air of an Arabian aristocrat, the playfulness of a boy and the intensity of a man, who made her realize that smoldering kisses should be a major food group. But Megan could never give him her heart....

#763 LET'S MAKE A BABY! by Jacqueline Diamond
To avoid an arranged marriage, Annalisa de la Pena needed to find a willing man who would father her child. Ryder Kelly was the man she chose. But Ryder wanted more than a fling—he wanted to know what Annalisa was hiding....

#764 FOR BETTER, FOR BACHELOR by Nikki Rivers
What do you get when world-famous foreign correspondent Marcus Slade comes to the tiny town of Birch Beach, Wisconsin? Trouble! Especially when small-town girl Rachel Gale snares his heart....

Look us up on-line at: http://www.romance.net